MONSTER

FROM THE

ABYSS

A NOVEL BY MICHAEL COLE

SEVERED PRESS
HOBART TASMANIA

MONSTER FROM THE ABYSS

Copyright © 2021 MICHAEL COLE

WWW.SEVEREDPRESS.COM

ISBN: 978-1-922551-75-7

CHAPTER 1

It had died recently.

In the three days since docking along the southwest bend, Roy Brinkman had discovered enough death to fill a cemetery. In fact, that was how he would describe the ocean floor surrounding Diamond Green—an underwater cemetery. The coral had turned black, the life that previously flourished now lying dead in the rocks.

Roy's throat tightened. He stood on the aft deck of his yacht *Europa*, unable to take his eyes off the twenty-foot corpse floating just twelve yards off the starboard quarter. In life, the humpback whale had reached a length of fifty-feet, and was a graceful mother. The tag near her left flipper confirmed she was the one the marine biologist had been tracking for fourteen months. There was no sign of the eight-month-old runt she was nursing.

He heard footsteps behind him.

"She tested positive," Brett Rollins said. Roy cocked his head just enough to see his twenty-five-year-old graduate student in his peripheral vision.

"Dioxin?"

"Yes, Doctor."

Roy sighed, then leaned against the guardrail. His hands strangled the metal bar as guilt and anger assaulted his mind. He had been part of the investigative team that exposed the White Flag Paper Mill for its illegal dumping of toxic waste in the Atlantic. Using high-powered submersibles, he conducted ten-thousand foot dives, roughly fifty-miles northeast of Key Largo. Over the next month, water testing showed traces of chemical presence, as though the leaked barrels had formed a river leading southwest toward the Keys.

Clearly, he didn't catch it in time. He had suspected the paper mill of devious activities in this region after one of their facilities in Maine had been caught spilling chlorine in a riverbed that ran through a timber wood forest. Here, at the private island of Diamond Green, it was the worst he'd ever seen. And it was only just beginning.

The humpback whale had been torn to shreds. A feeding frenzy, perhaps? In his ten years following dissertation, he had witnessed over two-hundred such events. He'd seen hammerheads, reef sharks, and blue sharks tear into schools of fish, the blood attracting others for miles. He watched crystal blue waters turn into clouds of chaos and red mist. But nothing compared to what must've happened here.

He had tested the flesh. This whale couldn't have been dead for more than a day. Yet, the flesh had nearly been stripped to the bone. There was just enough fatty tissue clinging to the skeleton to keep it afloat. It would take days of consistent feeding for even a large school of sharks to do such damage. Speaking of bone, he had yet to see anything that could sever a whale's spine. The lower half of its body was nowhere to be seen. In addition, on the little flesh that remained, there was no clear indication of teeth marks. Instead, it looked as though several buzzsaws had been taken to the poor creature.

It was drifting steadily to the south. By end of day, it would be nothing but a dot in the horizon.

"Had to have been sharks," Brett said. Roy shrugged. It was the only explanation that made sense. Perhaps his estimate on the time of death was wrong. He didn't think so, but nothing else made sense.

His temples felt as though an invisible force was compressing his skull.

"Everything that's taken a bite out of this thing is now carrying toxin. Then they will die, and their bodies will be eaten. Then those that eat them will pass it on. It will be an endless cycle of death, and not in the way nature intended."

Brett was soothing his own headache. "Perhaps we should call the E.P.A."

"They'll write it off as residue from the waste site," Roy replied. "We need to find clear evidence of a fresh source, if there even is any."

"Do you think there is?"

Roy nodded. "The reefs up in the northern Florida Valley didn't test this high. The readings show a spike here. We need to figure out where it's originating from."

He watched the clear blue waters. Gentle waves lapped at the hull. The water itself was clear as glass, the rock beds beneath entirely visible. He could see some fish swimming about, but Roy knew they should be in greater abundance than this.

Sadly, this phenomenon wasn't something that was isolated to this specific spot. Salmon, flounder, and several species of fish had been reported to be washing ashore along the Florida Coast. Fishermen had been reporting record low numbers along the Keys. In Key Largo, reports hit the web of two swimmers reporting fevers after swimming on the beaches.

To his right was the island of Diamond Green, a tiny speck of land in the middle of the stretch of blue. It was roughly a third-of-a-mile wide, home to two residences, the Instone property, and another which belonged to a relative.

Far to the north was Mr. Instone's fishing vessel. It was heading west to the mainland. Roy's curiosity piqued, naturally.

Wonder where he's going.

Usually, Mr. Instone fished further east. He was the one who initially informed Roy of the dead fish in the area. Perhaps he was trying a different location. Or perhaps, he was simply heading to the mainland for groceries or fuel. After all, living on a private island meant no Seven-Eleven stops.

Brett's voice snapped Roy from his trance.

"You going down for samples, Doctor?"

"You know you can call me Roy."

"Just being polite."

Roy snickered. "Yeah, I'll go. Gotta see if these dioxin levels are being transmitted by the sea life, or if that paper mill had more than one dumping ground. Is the Power Ray recharged?"

"In about twenty minutes. Still sounds like something from *Power Rangers* when you call it that."

Roy rolled his eyes. "Every time?"

"That's what it sounds like!"

"Sweet Jesus. What would you prefer I call it?"

"Just call it the PR," Brett said.

"Fine. You prep the *PR*, and I'll get set up. I just wish the damn institution would've let us keep our submersible."

"Want me to send out the drone while you're out?"

Roy thought about it a moment, then nodded. "Send it over to the north side of the island, and I'll check around here. Maybe we'll find some actual evidence today.

Before entering the cabin, Roy gave one last look at the whale corpse. A chill ran down his spine. *I'm not convinced that even a school of sharks would do this much damage.*

CHAPTER 2

Sicilia Instone stood on the pier, watching the birds gliding over the ocean. She couldn't remember the last time she stopped to watch the birds, or nature in general. She didn't truly appreciate the simple things in life until recently. The ocean breeze swept her blond hair, revealing shoulders as gold as the beach. She looked to the left, just in time to notice a few wandering glances turning away suddenly. The shores of Elliot Key were full of tourists picnicking and wallowing into the shallow waters, and more than once, a few male gazes turned toward her. At least they were attempting to be subtle about it, whether to save their own dignity, or to spare themselves the wrath of their wives. Sicilia cracked a thin smile. She enjoyed the sense of power her attractiveness granted her—more now than ever, now that the papers were finally signed. A year ago, she had to be careful not to be too flamboyant with her appearance. The memories of the resulting outbursts, some of which took place in public restaurants, easily eliminated that smile.

The bruises from divorce were almost worse than the physical ones that led to it. It was a life she put up with for ten years. The money was good. Great, even. But wealth only brings a certain degree of happiness. It doesn't substitute, or make up for, lack of affection, infidelity, and hot tempers. Even the hefty court settlement couldn't truly make up for the misery. Not just from the arguments, but from never truly being loved in the first place.

"Ms. Instone?"

It took the ferry attendant two attempts to get her attention. She hadn't gotten used to her maiden name yet. For the past decade, it was Mrs. Wellington.

"Pardon me," she said. She turned to face the short man dressed in a white shirt. His white shirt was soaked in sweat and his pants were wrinkled.

"It's okay, ma'am. We have your baggage all set. You sure you will be okay will all of this?" Sicilia looked at the section of pier behind the attendant. She had six briefcases and one large duffle bag stuffed with all of her belongings.

"Yes, I'll be fine."

"With respect, the harbor closes at ten. It almost looks like you're here to stay…"

"On the contrary, I'll be leaving in just a few minutes," Sicilia replied. She pointed to the ocean, specifically at a little dot in the horizon. Even from this distance, she recognized that rattling foghorn. The boat attendant saw the boat and nodded.

"Oh! Makes sense now. Going to Key Largo?"

"Nope. Somewhere much better," Sicilia said. That brought the smile back. Waves of nostalgia crept up her spine, giving her a burst of energy. She couldn't wait to return to Diamond Green. She was a much younger woman when she last saw it, eager to take advantage of her physical maturity. Her image on a hundred magazine covers, and specifically the money that came with it, quickly diluted the memories of family and belonging. She was thirty-one now, and while her figure remained mostly the same, her mind had finally matured. She was done making copious amounts of wealth. Now, she just wanted peace and quiet—to get away from the cameras. Yeah, the gazes were nice, until she remembered those gazers only saw flesh, and not the human being it cloaked. Same thing with Bill.

Perhaps that was another reason she was excited to hear that rusty foghorn. The man on board that fishing boat would not gaze at her in such a way. She could barely contain her excitement as the boat gradually became larger.

The same dirty rags hung from the crow's nest. Black fumes billowed from the smokestack, like something out of an old cartoon. The hull was painted solid white the last she saw the boat. Now, it flaked, exposing the black fiberglass layer between it and the steel. For some reason, she thought the flybridge stood higher than it really did. Distant memories clouded by a decade of adventures, heartbreak, and a vivid imagination were clearly to blame.

Standing at the helm was a towering figure. Sicilia waved to her Uncle Lucas, and smiled when she saw him wave back. A couple of minutes later, he brought his boat along the dock. The short beard matched those in her memories, aside from the fact that it was greyer. The hair on his head seemed to be retaining most of its black color. Then there were a few wrinkles on the face. But other than that, Uncle Lucas did not show any signs of slowing down. He had a physique most men in their twenties would kill for.

The boat smelled of fish, but Sicilia didn't care. She didn't bother waiting for him to hook up the mooring. Lucas had barely climbed down to the main deck when his niece practically leapt on him. Her arms practically choked him in their big hug.

"Oh my! Missed you too, kiddo!" he exclaimed.

"Hi, Uncle Lucas," Sicilia said. She finally let go.

"Nice to see you in person. The occasional texts weren't doing it for me."

"God, I'm sorry. You know the story," she said.

"Nah, don't be sorry, kid. Here, help me tie us on before we float away." The two of them uncoiled the mooring line and wrapped it around the nearest dock post. "When was the last time you've been on a boat? Not counting the trip over here."

"Every other fucking day, really," Sicilia said.

"Hey. Language!" Lucas said.

Sicilia chuckled. "Oh, for crying out loud, Uncle Lucas. I'm not ten years old anymore."

"In my eyes you will be. Almost got you a teddy bear to celebrate your return."

"I really appreciate you NOT doing that," Sicilia said. "And if you saw some of my photos, you'd see I've been surrounded by water and on boat decks two-thirds of my shoots."

"That's exactly it—I'd rather NOT see them. Little one, you *want* me to have a heart attack? I swear, the one you sent me from your first photo shoot...practically wearing nothing, just about made me join your dad."

She laughed. "Oh, for crying out loud. I wasn't wearing *nothing*."

"I said PRACTICALLY nothing. I swear, they make bikinis smaller than ever these days."

"Don't report me to the church elders."

"Young one, I practically AM the church elder. I'll tell you this much: seeing you, a grown woman, makes me feel older than Noah."

"You're still young," Sicilia said.

"I appreciate that," he said, flexing his bicep.

"Jesus! With arms like that, how the hell have you remained single all this time? I know a dozen women twenty years your junior that would be all over you!"

"I appreciate you telling me I'm still young, then in the next breath tell me about girls who are two decades younger than me," he replied.

Sicilia smiled. "Sorry. Still, you only live once! I could set you up an *Instagram* account. I guarantee you'd be hooking up in a month."

"Oh, Lord above, kid," he said. "You know I don't hook up. And I DEFINITELY don't go for that social media nonsense. World's immoral enough as it is."

"Hey now. It's not ALL bad. Certainly helped me make bank."

"Still glad you're out of that lifestyle. I hate knowing a bunch of filthy eyes are ogling you on the internet," he said.

"Oh, Uncle Lucas. The world isn't one big church."

"If only it was. Personally, I think life would be so much simpler," he replied. "Come on. Let's get all your stuff loaded."

They spent the next few minutes hauling her briefcases onto the vessel. Lucas scooped up the last two briefcases under his arms and plopped them on the deck.

"My goodness, sweetie, you packing bricks?"

"What? Too much for those big guns of yours to handle?" Sicilia said.

"I'm still an old man."

"Not even close," she said.

Lucas shrugged. "I might still have a while to go, yet." He smiled and hugged her again. "Glad to see you back, kiddo."

She squeezed him back. "How's the house?"

"Let's get out of here and you can see for yourself."

"Can I blow the horn like you'd let me do when I was a kid?"

Lucas sniggered then looked up, remembering all the old times. "Yes, of course."

"Woohoo!" Sicilia followed her uncle into the cockpit. The engine roared and the boat took off to the east, the horn blasting loudly for the first several minutes of the trip.

CHAPTER 3

After two hours of travel over open water, Sicilia Instone gazed at Diamond Green for the first time in ten years. A tiny speck of land, it still rivaled the rest of the Keys in terms of sheer beauty. Even from three-quarters-of-a-mile out, she could make out the silver palms lining the west shore. From her distance, she could see the entire stretch, which went from the north peak down to the southwest bend. On the western edge of the bend were three buccaneer palms overlooking the beach where she often played as a kid. With the boat slightly angled south, she could see the crooked slant of shore on the south side. Roughly two-hundred meters southeast, the shore dipped inward, forming Diamond Cove where the two houses were located. The sargassum smell wasn't too potent, much to her surprise, as the sea algae usually bunched up at the shores this time of year, creating that famous 'rotten egg' odor.

A tidal wave of memories came back to her. She looked to the north beach again and remembered nearly getting pinched by a stone crab. Almost every day during her childhood, she would walk up the western shore up to the north peak. From there, she'd travel down the crescent-shaped northeast shore to east point, then walk south from there to Uncle Lucas' house, which overlooked the ocean from the southeast peninsula. If he wasn't out fishing, she'd join him for a cup of tea and a game of volleyball on his beach. Then, she'd complete the walk, taking a turn at the tip of the peninsula, then walk northwest until ending up at her father's dock, located within the throat of Diamond Cove.

As often young people tired of things, her interest in the island's natural beauty began to wane once she entered her later teens. The island, which she thought of as freeing and liberating, was becoming a prison. She wanted to get out more. See more people. She felt a drive to enjoy typical things, such as mall shopping, moviegoing...maybe even earn some money herself. She hated the idea of college—homeschooling was enough of a drag. She couldn't imagine actually having to *pay* for education that she didn't care to have to begin with. But she wanted to see the world, and seeing the world wasn't cheap.

But there was always a way of getting someone to pay for the trip. She didn't have much talent, but she was all too aware of her golden skin, perfect hair, and pronounced feminine features—the perfect blend for modeling. How hard could it be to stand in front of a camera and pose? She loved exercise. Hell, she couldn't stay still for too long. And she enjoyed the attention. Still did…but not quite as much.

She thought of Bill. For a moment, the sense of nostalgia peeled away, bringing forth the aching feeling of being thought of only for her body. He didn't see past her skin, hair, breasts, womanhood, and didn't think much of her beyond the physical pleasure and the financial revenue she brought in. She was certainly good at selling boats, and being married to the marketing director of *Grand Craft Boats* ensured she'd always be available.

Sicilia shook her head, as though trying to physically rid herself of the memories. No need to think of the fat schlub. Had it not been for the three-hundred grand he made a year, along with the thirty-thousand dollar bonuses, he never would have attracted so much voluptuous female attention. The only good thing he ever provided was money. Hell, with the house paid for, and the company funding their many trips, she was able to essentially pocket the vast majority of her salary. That, along with the five-hundred-thousand dollar settlement, pretty much allowed her a life of luxury for a few years. Still, it didn't remove the sick feeling his name brought. Nor did it remove the guilt she felt. Guilt for not being around when her father passed away. Guilt for knowing he died knowing she was essentially being used by the company and its marketing director. Guilt for not helping when she found out he was in debt after purchasing a new fishing boat—which she now owned. It didn't matter that it was nearly paid off by the time she found out about it. She could've helped, and she didn't.

Hovering above it all like a thundercloud was the guilt for hardly calling him. She didn't take well to his objection to her marriage. Only now, with the benefit of age, wisdom, and hindsight, did she realize that it wasn't modeling he opposed, but the people she was working for specifically. There were no reported scandals or controversies—it was just that he simply *knew* a scoundrel when he saw one. And, as usual, he was right. She just wished he were here to see her turn to the light.

Damn it! She squeezed her eyes shut.

"You alright?"

She turned around, leaning back on the bow rail to look up at the cockpit. Her frustration must've been more obvious than she thought, judging by the concern displayed in Uncle Lucas' eyes and voice.

"Oh, nothing. Just wish *he* was here."

"Me too," Lucas replied. "Still have me, though, kiddo."

"Yes. Thank you, God," she replied. She was amazed at the power that little exchange held. Uncle Lucas was her only remaining family, and she loved him dearly. In a way, spending quality time with him would somewhat make up for lost time with her father. The two of them were inseparable growing up. So much so, that they continued living on their private island, as their fathers did before them, and theirs before them, and so on.

Sicilia gazed at the island some more. As they drew closer, she could see some of the lush green growing in the rocky interior. The bench on the southwest cove wasn't there anymore. Nor was the little playset.

"Hey! What happened to all the—"

"Storm damage," Uncle Lucas said, knowing by the tone of her voice what she was asking. "Not like there's any young ones to enjoy the swing set anymore."

"Fuck, I've never outgrown swing sets," she said.

"What did I say about language, young lady?"

Sicilia smiled. "Sorry, Uncle." She folded her arms over the rail and watched the island seemingly grow larger. She was already feeling the temptation to dive along the coral beds. With some luck, she'd get to swim alongside a sea turtle, or get to inspect starfish resting along the reefs. She had swum with blue sharks at least a dozen times, as well as pods of dolphins and even Orcas.

However, a few things did not quite match her recollection. The coral reef wasn't nearly as vibrant as she remembered in the shallow areas. She wondered if they were just too far out, or if her imagination made the reefs seem more colorful than they actually were. She shook her head. That couldn't be the case. She remembered standing on the beach and looking out to the southwest shore. On a clear sunny day, the Venus sea fans would turn a shade of purple as they collected plankton. Being nutrient rich waters, the little atoll was surrounded by all kinds of soft coral, which in turn provided habitats for fish.

Sicilia kept a watchful eye on the shallows as Lucas steered the vessel south. Her enthusiasm for returning home faded slightly. She could barely see the reef. There were few vivid colors. In fact, what she could see didn't look appealing at all. She saw white. White meant death for coral.

"You're probably wondering about *him*," Lucas said.

"Huh? Who?" Sicilia said. Had she been looking straight ahead, she would've seen the research vessel anchored a quarter mile southeast. It was about the size of a sword-fishing boat. Maybe eighty feet in length. She thought she could see movement on deck, but couldn't make out what the crew was doing, or even how many of them there were.

"Marine biologist. Dr. Roy Brinkman," Lucas said.

"Fascinating," Sicilia said. "What's he doing *here*?" She looked back at her uncle.

"I was going to tell you," Lucas said.

"Tell me what? Did something happen?" she asked.

"You've heard about the paper mill, right?"

Sicilia shook her head. "I've been busy with *other things*, Uncle Lucas." He nodded. He couldn't blame her for not keeping up with the news. Hell, *he* didn't care to keep up with it half the time. Then again, the poor internet reception out here often absolved him of the so-called duty to be informed—or at least, what the talking heads considered to be 'informed.'

"They were caught illegally dumping toxic waste."

"Really? Where?"

"Roughly fifty-miles northeast of here," Lucas said.

"Is that why--?"

"I've spoken with the doctor on occasion. He claims the toxin levels have increased drastically in our area."

"All over the Keys?"

"Yes, but it's especially bad around here," Lucas said. "*I* specifically notified the Coast Guard when I was hauling in all kinds of dead fish. They notified the EPA, who notified some institution, who sent him."

"Wait—how bad has fishing been?" she asked.

"Bad."

"Uncle?"

He knew the tone. It was a question and accusation all at once. Lucas wasn't about to do the song-and-dance of debating whether he had enough funds for supplies. The house was completely paid for, as it was passed down. But there were always repairs needed, as well as the cost of fuel for the boat, and having the propane tanks refilled every so often. Most of all, there was the expense of having underwater power cables installed and connected to the nearest junction, which was by no means a cheap venture.

"I'm fine. *We're* fine. You live here now. Again. Praise be to God."

"Amen," she said. "Still, I'm able to help financially."

Lucas pretended to frown. "Pay your own utilities. Now that we've got those cables, you oughta be able to do it through the internet. Isn't that the popular way to do things, nowadays?"

"You make it sound like a bad thing."

"Being void of human contact isn't necessarily a good thing."

Sicilia laughed. "Says the guy living on a private island."

"Didn't always live alone," he said. "And with you back, I won't be alone anymore."

"Not like we're living in the same house," she said.

"You're close enough," he replied. "And soon, I hope you'll marry someone good, who also loves the sea. More specifically, someone who'll care for you and love you properly."

She laughed again. It was obvious it pained him to say that, as it was difficult for him to acknowledge she was not a little girl anymore, even at her age.

"Don't need taken care of," she replied.

"Oh, for heaven's sake. I can't stand this modern age. You ladies somehow associate 'being taken care of' as some kind of weakness. It's not; it's about giving yourself to someone, and that person doing the same to you. Hence, God calls it a union."

Sicilia's first instinct was to make some sort of sarcastic remark, but she managed to hold back. Though intended as humor, it likely wouldn't be received well, and she didn't want to make her reunion with her beloved uncle awkward. Plus, she couldn't deny feeling a little of the intended effectiveness. How could she judge marriage when hers failed so miserably? Yeah, she got a good chunk of money out of the deal, but how could she explain her emptiness? Still, it was like pulling teeth to admit he might be right.

She thought of Uncle Lucas and Aunt Mary and how inseparable they were. She hoped their wedding photos were still on her bookcase. Despite the luxury of living on a private island, they were never rich, at least not financially. If anything, Sicilia was by far the wealthiest of anyone in their long running family tree. Yet, she was the unhappiest.

She turned around to look at him again. "Is Dad's boat still there?"

"Of course not," Lucas said. "He made it specifically clear that everything that was once his is now yours. That includes the boat."

That nearly brought a tear to her eye. "Gosh. It's so surreal being back."

"I'm happy to have you back," Lucas said. "You remember how to operate the boat?"

"I haven't even *seen* it. It's the new one Dad bought after his engine broke down."

"It's the same in every way. You'll see when you get there."

Sicilia watched the shore as they passed the southwest corner of the island. She was tapping the guardrail with excitement now. She could almost see the beach just a little ways to the east. The concern and disappointment she felt when seeing the dying reef faded for now. Nostalgia consumed her. Her veins flowed with an energy she hadn't felt since *leaving*, ironically. The rocky shores of the inner southeast peninsula came into view. As Lucas completed the turn, she finally laid eyes on the house she grew up in.

"Welcome home," he said.

This time, a tear managed to break free.

"Glad to be back."

CHAPTER 4

For a moment, Sicilia was ten years old again. Aside from a fresh coat of paint, the house looked almost exactly the same. The front yard was a thirty-degree hill that ran twenty feet to a long stretch of yard.

Standing up on the dock, she almost expected her father to peer out through the second floor bedroom window, just like he used to when she would play on the sand beach. She put a hand on the gunwale of his fishing boat. Cigar stubs lined the inner edges of the deck. She could almost smell the Dominican tobacco that Dad smoked when fishing. Though this boat was only five years old, the signs of use indicated that it was practically his second home. The paint was already chipped, the bulkheads stained with ash, the stern still wreaking of bait. The nets were still hooked up to the outriggers. It was clear that Uncle Lucas hated the thought of tampering with the boat too much. When maintaining it, he mainly focused on engine function, as well as testing the winch, fueling it, and making sure all the gears were in place. He didn't clean it—it'd be like wiping away the last traces of his brother. And Sicilia had no desire to, either.

To her left was the fifteen-foot skiff. The outboard motor was still attached, with a tarp placed over it to protect it from the elements. Once again, she was flooded with memories. That was the boat she used as a kid when she would go snorkeling. It had been so long since she swam freely, with nothing but the water and its inhabitants to accompany her.

The thought brought her eyes back to the ocean. Already, she felt the urge to take a dive out near the north peak. Her mind ran with the idea, leading to the self-imposed challenge to take the speargun out and catch herself a wahoo or even an amberjack.

She turned her gaze toward her uncle, who smiled at her from the flybridge of his boat. He climbed down to the main deck and began unloading her luggage. Sicilia took two briefcases and proceeded down the dock. There were three wooden steps leading to the sand. To her right was a large rock bed that lined the inner part of the southeast peninsula. She was overwhelmed. Why hadn't she come back sooner?

With Uncle Lucas right behind her, she proceeded up the hill, her toes squelching the sand with each step. She had been to hundreds of beaches in her travels, but this one simply felt unique. The only word she could think to describe it was 'welcoming'.

The beach ended a couple of meters before the foot of the hill. It was a short and easy climb to the top. She could see past the house to the island interior. It was a world of rocks, clay-colored hills, and buccaneer palms. Beyond that, it was a background of blue sky and specks of ocean.

She hesitated before opening the screen door. The handle was still slightly bent, as it always was. Dad always said it wasn't broken, which Mom argued that it was. Looks like he was right, because there it was, still holding on. She gently clutched the little brown lever and pushed it down. The doorlatch released, the hinges groaning slightly as it opened.

Her bare feet felt the threads of the old cardigan rug. She expected the room to be smaller than in her memory. In fact, it seemed *larger*. Probably because one of the chairs was missing, making the center of the room more open. Dad had gotten rid of it a few years after Mom died. Having a companion chair with its rightful owner nowhere around was depressing. There were a few other differences. Dad had caught up with the 21st Century by finally replacing that old box tv with a smart tv. A fifty-five inch one too!

She passed through the room, glancing at the fireplace. There was fresh wood stacked nearby, courtesy of her uncle. Through the hallway, she saw the kitchen, dining area, and utility room. Everything had been freshly mopped and organized. There were even fresh groceries in the refrigerator and pantry.

"Oh, Uncle Lucas. You make me feel like a queen."

"You *are* royalty to me, kiddo," he replied. "That said, mind picking up the pace. You might think I'm muscly, but I'm not *Captain America*."

"What?! Well, my image of you is forever tattered!" Near the back door was a stairway that led upstairs. She deliberately took her time up the first few steps, until her uncle bumped her rear with his knee.

"Smart aleck."

She laughed and raced upstairs. She took a glance into the master bedroom. It was the only room where the appearance was greatly altered.

"I wasn't sure which room you'd want to sleep in," he said. "I prepared your old bedroom first, but I thought it seemed kind of small for an adult, so I cleaned out this one. I safely stored away some of your dad's stuff in my shed. The rest is in your attic. The photos and stuff I arranged around the house." Sicilia stood, unsure of what to do. Her instinct was to go to her old room. It seemed wrong to take her parents' bed. But, then again, she was the new head of the household.

She entered the master bedroom. The mattress was new. Memory foam. Dad had said something before about his arthritis making it hard to sleep. She hoped that this mattress served him well in his final couple of years. She sat on it. Extremely comfortable indeed. Of course, it was nothing new to her. Living a life of luxury—financially speaking—she had access to excellent furniture and appliances.

After placing the briefcases beside the bed, Uncle Lucas backed out into the hallway. "There you go, kiddo. I'll leave you to sort all that out the way you want it."

"You mean you won't help me put away my bras?" she joked. Right on cue, Uncle Lucas winced.

"You're the death of me, hon."

She gave him a hug. "Thanks for the lift."

"You betcha. Let me know if you need anything else. I'll leave you to get situated." He headed for the stairs.

"What'll you be up to?" Sicilia asked.

"I'm gonna take the boat east. Gotta try and catch *something*. Markets don't close because of a *little* toxin spill."

"How bad *is* it, exactly?" she asked.

Uncle Lucas stopped, then looked back. "Two days ago, I caught four pounds of mackerel over at the south trench. Bottom trawling. Most were already dead when I brought them aboard. I spoke with the marine biologist yesterday. He's been diving around the reefs lately. The fish populations have been dying out. Something's killing them off."

"So, there *is* another dumping site near here," Sicilia said.

"That's what he suspects. Though, I'd think I'd be able to spot any vessel traveling through here with suspicious cargo."

"But you've seen *nothing*?"

Uncle Lucas shook his head. "No. It's like this dioxin stuff just traveled here on its own. Unless they came in with a submarine, which I highly doubt. Anyways, I gotta get going. See you later, kid."

"Bye!"

After watching him disappear, she returned to the bedroom. She spent the next half hour sorting out all of her belongings. Luckily, everything was already divided in the suitcases, which saved her time in figuring out which items went where. The last item she waited on was a small duffle bag which contained her swimsuits. It was as though the sight of them had heightened her senses. She could suddenly hear the waves breaking apart on the rocks. The sound was so clear, she thought she was standing out in the yard again.

It had only been a half hour since she was away from the water—if it could even be considered 'being away'. The shore was only a few hundred feet away. Too far.

Sicilia hurried downstairs and stepped outside. The sense of longing made sense now. It wasn't simply a longing for the ocean, but for these specific shorelines. The rocks, the peninsulas, the cove... ALL of Diamond Green. She felt a sense of peace that she couldn't describe. This place, that she couldn't wait to escape from as a kid, she now wanted to cherish forever.

What better way to begin that appreciation than to take one of her walks around the shores?

She started west, splashing her feet along the water line as she moved toward the southwest bend. Her nostalgia was bitten once again by a mild sense of disappointment. The rounded piece of shore seemed empty without the little playset and seat benches. She wasn't much of a carpenter, but already, she was having thoughts of building something there. Perhaps she could goad Uncle Lucas into building something. He was fairly handy with tools. If not, she would special order one. As for the playset, she couldn't deny she was too old for that. Still, it felt wrong not having one here.

Sicilia walked along the shore, which eventually took her northeast. She walked the half-mile distance between the southwest bend and the north peak, gazing at each tree as she went. She was surprised to see the one with the crooked trunk still there. In the few seasons before her departure, it was showing signs of decay. However, it still stood, looking better than ever. The one next to it, however, was gone. It had been struck by lightning, which severely burned the base of the trunk. Her dad suspected the burn impaired the tree's ability to absorb water. Otherwise, this beach was the same as ever. The sand was white-tan, which was visible under the water for several yards.

Looking out to the ocean, she couldn't help but notice again the lack of vivid colors where she normally saw the reefs. Was her memory just playing tricks on her? Possibly, though Lucas had said something about the toxins affecting the waters.

It was when she arrived at the north peak that a barrage of memories returned all at once. The north peak was almost a perfect arrow-shape stretch of land, literally the tip of the island. There was a small dock extending from the eastern side. It was still there, well-maintained by the island's single inhabitant. She remembered the first time she caught an Atlantic salmon off the edge of that dock. Her dad stood right beside her, guiding her on how to bring it in.

Her eyes went from the outer edge to the supports on the right side. She would tie a mooring line whenever they brought the skiff in after diving. Whenever they needed to set foot on shore to either take a break or check equipment, they'd return to this dock, rather than go all the way around the island to the cove.

While gazing at the water, Sicilia formed a half-fist with her right hand. In her imagination, she was holding the grip of her dad's speargun, ready to put the projectile through the side of an anglerfish. She remembered bursting from the water, holding the tether which held her prize. Then, of course, her dad made her gut it. Had to learn *everything*. Can't have daddy do all the real work. She remembered hating it at the time. Now, she wondered if she could still pull it off.

With that memory came another call from the ocean. It was like a lover enchanting her to join it. To become one. And that call was becoming irresistible.

Did Dad save the diving gear?

She hoped so, because she was going into that water one way or another. Like a soldier on a mission, she moved down the crescent-shaped shore connecting the north peak to the east point. More sand, more rocks, all nostalgic. But nothing beat the sight of walking down to the southeast peninsula and seeing Uncle Lucas' house. It was two-stories, like hers. The dock was a little larger, to which, Lucas would joke to her father that 'my dock is bigger than your dock.' She chuckled. As a kid, she didn't get the humor, but now that she was grown up, she was laughing for a different reason. It was probably the only crude thing Uncle Lucas had ever said, and if she were to ever mention it, he'd play dumb about his awareness of the metaphor.

Unfortunately, his boat wasn't there, meaning he was out fishing. She knew that upon arrival. Still, it sucked. She wouldn't mind having a cup of tea or coffee. And the volleyball net was still there. In fact, it looked remarkably clean. She approached it and examined the stakes. There was soil bunched up around them. He had just recently set this up.

He remembered. Without his niece here, there wasn't much reason to keep it up. But now, things were different. Tomorrow morning, she'd complete her walk and conclude it with their usual routine.

At least, she hoped so.

Looking out to the eastern horizon, she couldn't miss the dark line of clouds. With the beauty of the ocean also came her wrath. It was nature's way of reminding humans of just how small they really were. And there was no doubt that the ocean was intent on reminding her later on tonight. She had to take the good with the bad. To enjoy such peaceful moments of serenity like this, she had to endure the days of rolling waves and screaming winds.

"Fuck." She quickly cupped a hand over her mouth and looked around, then shook her head. *He's out fishing.* She laughed at herself, then continued walking the shore, though this time with increased pace. Her desire was to get in that water, and with that storm coming in, it was clear that she had a limited window of time to dive today. And there was no way she'd sleep without diving.

For a moment, she considered simply moving inland. All she would have to do was walk across the peninsula and she'd be right there in Diamond Cove. But no, she still wanted to complete her normal walk. She'd just have to rush it. She followed the shore to the tip of the southeast peninsula, then skipped over the rocky inner shore as she made her way into the cove. Then it was back up the hill to the house.

She was grateful she took the time to do that. Better than spending her first hours back home sorting out laundry and toiletries. And the best was yet to come. She walked around the side yard to the storage shed.

"Please be in there," she said. She opened the doors, and to her relief, she saw the diving suits and scuba tanks. She checked the gauges on the canisters. They were replenished and ready to go. "Yes!" She tested the rebreathers then held up the harnesses. Should fit her perfectly. The suits were on a rack on her left-hand side. She checked one that was her mother's. Again, she almost cried. It was as though Dad had left it here for her to find. She was the same size as her mother was. Looked a lot like her too. Same hair color, same slim cheekbone structure, while her Greek nose was all her dad's genetics.

As she collected the gear, she stopped at the sight of a heavy metal case in the back. The best was yet to come. *Is that...* She dragged the case toward her and opened it. There lay the speargun she and Dad used in her childhood. Another "Yes!" escaped her lungs. She hurried to the house with the diving gear wrapped in her arms like a newborn. Right there in the living room, she stripped, replacing her clothes with her diving suit. She tied her hair into a ponytail, then tested the goggles. The flippers fit well and were in good condition.

Now, it was time to go out and catch herself a fish. A devious grin formed on her face. Nothing would be more hilarious than her bringing in a nineteen-pound snapper after being told the fish had moved out of the region.

She returned to the shed, grabbed the speargun case, and a knife. If the fish didn't die, she'd have to put it out of its misery. She remembered the first time she stabbed a fish in the head. It took more effort than her dad made it look, and the *crunch* almost made her nauseous. Today, though, she was feeling up to it. Perhaps it was Dad's spirit coursing through her. Maybe she was too amped up on good feelings and memories. Regardless, she felt powerful. Now, it was time to get out there and hunt a damn fish.

She piled her gear into the skiff, started the engine, then set course for the north peak.

CHAPTER 5

Doctor Roy Brinkman downed his water bottle. His muscles were tense, not from the swimming, but from the hauling of the hundred-pound mass that he brought aboard the *Europa*. His assistant, Brett, stood across from him, staring down at the finless blue shark that lay dead at his feet.

"Looks like we've got more problems around here than just toxic waste," he said.

"No shit," Roy replied. "You hear a lot about this taking place on the east coast. Not here though. At least, I never thought so."

"You think there's Asian markets around here?"

"I think they fly in here, make handshake agreements with local fishermen, then arrange to meet every-so-often to make the trade," Roy said. He groaned in frustration. The shark couldn't have been dead much longer than a day. Any longer than that, there'd hardly be enough to identify it as an animal, even with all the fish dying out. There were plenty of lacerations along its underside, mostly from crabs and lobsters chipping away at it. But the gash along its nose was enough for Roy to know the poor animal had been hooked. It was hauled out of water by human hands, which proceeded to slice its fins off, then toss the now eel-shaped animal into the water to drown.

Brett ran his fingers through his hair. "You don't think Mr. Instone would—"

"Hell no," Roy said. "Not a chance in hell."

"Well, we've only known him for a few days. Can we really be sure?"

"It would take a special kind of idiot to dump a shark's body on your own front door, where scientists are making non-stop dives to inspect the area. No, I think it's fairly obvious whose work this is."

"The Glasses? You think they'd come out this far?"

"Dude? Where've you been lately? We saw them *two days* ago!"

"Oh, that was *them*?! I thought that was someone else," Brett said. "I guess I'm used to them harassing us whenever they come by."

"Maybe they were too busy," Roy said, looking down at the dead shark.

"You think they did *that* too?" Brett asked. Roy turned to his right at a net containing the mangled remains of another shark. There wasn't much to go on, just the head, neck, and part of the dorsal and pectoral fin.

He shrugged his shoulders. "Hard to tell with that one. I can see those idiots butchering it for fun. But, they'd at least take the fins. And there's too much there that they would've let go to waste. And there's no delicacy for shark meat other than the fins."

Still, it didn't make sense. The injury didn't match that of a shark bite. Rather, it almost looked as though a giant pair of weed cutters had cut through the thing. And the head—had there not been a mouth lined with a few remaining teeth, he wouldn't have known he was looking at a shark head. It had been crushed, as though caught in a huge compactor.

"Where'd you find it?" Brett asked.

"Near the south trenches," Roy said. "I gotta get in touch with the institution. I need that damn submersible back. It's too deep to dive over there. And I doubt that jackass Dr. Wayans will relinquish it. He's having too much fun taking babes for a ride near Key West."

"Good to have seniority," Brett said, chuckling.

"Seniority, and to kiss the chairman's ass apparently," Roy said.

"True." Brett looked down at the dead shark and the heap of tattered flesh that used to be a shark. "So...were you planning on testing these?"

"Yes," Roy said. "Now that we likely have people poaching in this area, we need to make sure they're not selling food that's loaded with toxic waste. That, and if that one got eaten by something, then we have a fairly large animal somewhere in these waters that's now infected." He pulled his flippers off and tossed them aside. "Did the drone pick up anything?"

"Nothing peculiar. I have it drifting on the north side," Brett said.

"Let me take a look. I doubt we'll find anything this shallow."

They stepped into the interior of the vessel. A small stairway led them below deck into the lab. Roy bit his lip, refraining from commenting on the mess that was the lab tables. The microscopes hadn't been put back where they belonged, nor the testing kits used after Brett examined the tissue samples taken from the dead whale.

They moved to the computer table on the forward end. On the monitor was a glistening blue image from sunlight piercing shallow water.

Roy took a seat and seized the joystick. "Where is it, exactly?"

"Near Buoy Five," Brett said. Roy angled the drone near the surface.

"Oh, yes. Now I see it." He angled the drone downward. It was nearly two-hundred and fifty-feet deep around here. He suspected that the dumping site, assuming there was one, was further out. But he needed a damn submersible to properly examine the area. Still, with the evident effects on the sea life, there was still a chance that the source was somewhere nearby.

"I've already been around this spot, boss," Brett said. "It's all on footage if you'd like to look at it."

"Or I could just drive the thing around myself and save a little time," Roy said. Brett leaned forward and tapped on the monitor. Roy felt slightly embarrassed when he saw the battery icon starting to blink. "Oh…"

"You know, boss, you CAN trust me if you feel like it."

Roy cringed slightly. The words were spoken humorously, but clearly cushioning his true feelings.

"My bad, Brett," he said. He looked at the vial-shaped icon. "Still, there's at least a half-hour to go."

"Yeah, and you'll need that time to bring the thing back," Brett said.

"It doesn't take a half hour for that," Roy said. "I just wanna get a look at something. Get it out of my system. Then I'll bring it back here." He steered the machine southwest. He checked another tab on the monitor to make sure he was nearing Buoy Four's location.

"You're getting further into the shallows," Brett said.

"I'm aware." After several minutes, Roy steered the drone further into the coral reef. In the few minutes that followed, they watched as it passed over a colony of great star coral. Golden in color, these specimens were fairly healthy, though some were starting to take on a more bleached color. "These weren't like this a few days ago." He then passed over some antler-shaped staghorn coral. So far, they kept their natural vibrant purple color.

"Nothing really to note with those. What are you looking for? It'll take time before we see significant change in this section of the reef," Brett said.

"*That.*" Roy pointed at the center screen. There was an array of dead fish littering the sea floor, many of them in various stages of decay. Some were fresh kills, fully intact from nose to tail, while others were being gnawed at by crustaceans...the ones that were still alive.

Brett cursed under his breath. It was like looking at an underwater gravesite. "Holy shit. We checked this spot yesterday. These dead fish weren't there."

"Exactly."

"So, what happened then? For these fish to have died *right here*, there had to be some sort of exposure in this exact spot."

"That's what I'm curious about," Roy said. He took the drone near the bottom, then weaved around the forest and staghorn coral and anemones.

"Should I get ahold of the EPA?"

Roy shook his head. "You'd think a bunch of dead fish would be enough, but unfortunately those knuckleheads won't come this far out unless they have concrete evidence of dumping." He sighed. "Of course, they have us out here to find evidence without the proper equipment." The blinking icon turned red. "Goddamn it. I better bring this thing back."

"Hey, I saw something," Brett said. "Something moving, along the corner there."

"Which corner?"

"Right! Right!" He watched the camera angle up. "No. *Lower* right!"

"Could've used that information before," Roy groaned. He accelerated and angled the camera downward.

"There! What is that?"

Roy had it dead center in the screen. The image was too murky, and the tentacles of an anemone were in the way. Whatever it was it was moving, and with frantic motion. At first, he thought it was a shark. Then he saw the caudal fin 'split' into two legs, which paddled up and down. A split-second later, he saw the air tank.

"A diver," Brett said. "A *woman.*"

Roy shook his eyes. "Barely identified it as a human, and the first thing you check is the rack."

Brett cocked a grin. "Hey, can you blame me? I mean, can't see much else… except that?!"

Roy looked back to the screen just in time to see the rifle-shaped object in her hand point at the screen. There was a rush of water, then suddenly the image turned black.

"Oh shit," Brett muttered.

CHAPTER 6

The boat rocked as the anchor struck the water. The line went taut, securing the skiff to the reef below. Sicilia rolled her shoulders and stretched her arms. It was obvious she was a little out of practice. The wetsuit was snug against her body, which was good, she just had to remember how to get used to the feel of a 'second skin'. The weight belt felt a little more natural, as she wore them constantly in the gym. Only this time, it was to help to control her buoyancy during her hunt.

She cleared the fog from her goggles and placed them over her eyes. Her scuba tank was strapped to her back, the harness clipped over her waist and chest. She remembered the first time she wore one. Back then, the thirty-five-pound cannister seemed heavy. Now, she was a strong woman who could give Dwayne Johnson a run for his money in an arm-wrestling match. At least, that's what she told herself. Regardless, the tank's weight was hardly noticeable for the adult diver, even though she was somewhat out of practice.

Sicilia wore a belt, to which the knife was secured over her weight belt. Though she never had a deadly shark encounter, it was always good to have something to defend herself with should one get a little too close. The blade was freshly sharpened, confirmed by a test against a spare piece of rope, which it sliced through like butter. She was certain she wouldn't need it, mainly because of her previous diving experiences, and because of her first line of defense.

She picked up the one-meter speargun. It felt a lot lighter than it looked. The barrel was made of mahogany, with a black rubber grip. The shaft itself was eight millimeters in diameter. She gripped the handle with one hand while using the other to pull the band. Positioning the handle near her chest, she pulled the band closer. *Click!* The speargun was loaded.

"Alright, let's do this," she said to herself. She placed the rebreather in her mouth. The air was warm and moist, thanks to the chemical reaction in the CO_2 scrubber. She was grateful, as it prevented her mouth from drying out. Keeping the spear-tip pointed away from her, she swung herself over the gunwale and hit the water. For a moment, she was surrounded by frothing water.

She took a few inhales from her rebreather. It felt at first like she wasn't getting enough oxygen, but in fact, that wasn't the case. After a few more inhales, it felt more natural. Stroking her legs, she let the weight guide her down the forty-foot depth. It wasn't so heavy that she couldn't swim. She kept the descent slow, pausing every few meters. She was glad for the pauses, because it served as a reminder to do so on her way up to the surface, which was a little more important for depressurization.

The water at this depth was a greenish blue. Her movements felt free and limited at the same time. She could only describe it as being in another world. Except, this strange world was so familiar.

She was diving two-hundred yards off the western side of the north peak. And like the landmarks on Diamond Green, all the familiarities of the ocean floor came back to her. She immediately saw the twin rocks, two enormous boulders that seemed fused together, overlooking a small shelf of reef. There were two anemones growing on the north side of them. They looked healthy enough. So did the brownish-colored brain coral nearby. There were a few fish swimming by, though not as many as there should be. Uncle Lucas was right; something was going on here. Back in the day, it took forever to get a decent photo of her and Dad posing underwater, because so many fish would get in the way. Now, the water seemed empty.

The speargun suddenly felt like dead weight. She felt foolish for bringing it along.

Relax. You've only been diving for three minutes.

With that in mind, she swam ahead and began exploring the western reefs. Unfortunately, her feelings didn't improve. Especially when she saw the white color of dying coral.

Elkhorn coral, shaped like elk antlers, were breaking apart with the slightest brush of water. A few dead crabs lay belly up nearby. There were only a few fish swimming about, mostly little ones. Lettuce-shaped coral was breaking apart like dried paint, the fragments littering the ocean floor. More white shapes stretched from the reef. It was like looking at an army of ghosts rising from the seabed. Dead seaweed clung to the rocks.

Sicilia was now feeling slightly nauseous. She wondered if it was even healthy for her to be swimming in this water. She wasn't ingesting it, but she still wondered if whatever was killing the fish and the coral could possibly affect her skin. Probably not, or else Uncle Lucas would've warned her about it. It wasn't like he didn't get wet from fishing, and he didn't look sick at all.

Besides, her curiosity was getting the better of her. She needed to know how bad the spread was.

She passed over several more meters of reef. Some of the shallower coral seemed okay, but those in the deeper regions seemed worse. And the fish population remained the same— practically nonexistent.

Sinking to a shelf in the reef, she sat down, holding the speargun as though posing as an 80's action hero. She stared at the field of death all around her. In less than an hour, she went from being incredibly happy to be home to being saddened. Before today, she was never told this was happening, and it hurt to see it for herself. Sadness wasn't the only emotion, however. She kept that speargun pointed outward, not just out of general safety, but out of self-preservation. She was feeling uncomfortable in these near-empty waters, as though something was watching her out beyond her field of view.

One thing was for sure: there wasn't anything worth hunting here. She turned to her right, grazing a healthy patch of seaweed. She pushed herself off the shelf with her feet, only for her slipper to get snagged on something. She jolted, feeling something snake-like covering her foot. She knelt down over the rocky shelf and shone her small waterproof flashlight at the object. It was dark black in color, several inches in diameter, and seemed to run forever along the ocean floor. Looking over her shoulder, she could see that it went all the way up to the island.

Then it dawned on her—the power lines that Uncle Lucas told her about.

Oh, shit. The natural fear of being electrocuted sank in. Had it not been for the thick patch of weeds covering this section of cable, she would've easily spotted it. The cable seemed to run northwest, where she assumed it connected with an island juncture a few miles off. Her foot had slid under it when she turned to move. She knelt down with caution, then slowly gripped the cable. It had a decent amount of weight to it, but she was able to lift it high enough to free her foot. She dropped it, collected her speargun, then elevated a few feet.

With the relief came the sense of foolishness. Obviously, underwater cables were more secure than that, but then again, she was no electrician. All she knew was that cables like these carried a high-voltage of electricity, and that electricity and water were not good bedfellows.

The tension returned as something bumped her hard from behind. As she reeled forward, a second impact struck her. This time, it felt like something had ahold of her tank. She endured a brief shake before that hold ceased abruptly. There was movement in the corner of her left eye.

Sicilia spun to the left, speargun pointed. She caught a glimpse of her attacker. A mighty caudal fin thrashed back and forth, pushing the mass of a twelve-foot mako shark. Her heart thumped wildly, adrenaline causing her to shake.

She wasn't alone in these waters after all!

Sicilia steadied herself, watching the shark circle around the coral beds. It grazed the seabed, examined the husk of a dead crab with its mouth, spat it out, then proceeded to circle around. The poor shark looked somewhat malnourished. These were likely its normal feeding grounds which she assumed it hunted all of its life. Now, there was a food shortage, causing it to go after anything that moved.

It dawned on her right then that she was technically the survivor of a shark attack. Not a title she expected to achieve from this casual little dive. She examined herself. Luckily, there were no injuries. She then checked her tank. There were a few marks leftover from the bite, but nothing serious. She resecured the harness, then watched the shark some more.

It kept its distance, likely unaccustomed to attacking such large prey. Also, it probably didn't like the taste and feel of her tank. It probably lost a tooth or two from the bite. Sicilia was grateful it didn't go for her leg. That sense of good luck faded quickly as the shark made another turn.

Stay over there.

She was aware of her heartbeat, which the fish undoubtedly could sense. It knew she was a living thing, made from flesh and blood. The sickly-looking shark moved in closer, cautiously at first, but gradually picking up speed.

Sicilia knew she couldn't outswim it. This was a starving predator. It would keep coming at her unless she *convinced* it to stay away. Fleeing was not only futile, but it would spur the shark on.

She let herself sink to the ledge, then crouched slightly. She pointed her speargun and awaited the shark's approach. At fifteen feet, its eyes rolled back. Its mouth opened. It closed the distance in the blink of an eye.

Sicilia thrust the speargun like a javelin. The tip punctured the shark's snout, drawing blood. It shook, freeing itself, then turned away. Sicilia jabbed it again for good measure, poking it along the gills. The shark darted away, quickly disappearing into the distance.

The diver relaxed, keeping a watchful eye on the distance in case the fish decided to make another run at her. She could see it swimming to the right, a couple hundred feet away. A few minutes passed, during which it remained at bay.

She was surprised that she didn't feel scared. Frankly, she felt somewhat rejuvenated. She was always told she was a thrill-seeker at heart, though she never thought she'd get such a feeling from a deadly shark encounter. There was a feeling of sadness for the creature, however. It definitely looked on the skinny side and her general understanding of sharks was that they didn't typically attack humans. If they did, it was commonly due to mistaken identity. Or in this case, starvation which led to desperation.

Regardless, it was a reminder that the reef was dying, its inhabitants having relocated or died. Feeling depressed, Sicilia decided to return to the skiff.

She hauled herself aboard and sat down behind the console. Dripping water from her hair, she removed her goggles and hoisted the anchor. She started the motor and turned the boat back toward the dock.

Sicilia slowed it to first gear, then stopped. As the boat rocked with the gentle waves, she stared at the ocean. From up here, it looked clean. Deceptive. And despite being deceptive, it still had a calming effect. All of a sudden, her mood lifted, and she was feeling another drive to dip back in.

"Swim, don't swim, nah, I want to swim. I must be going clinically insane," she muttered. She laughed at herself. First dive in, and already she was attacked by a damn shark! She should've been quivering with fear! Instead, she felt more energized than ever. Cautious, but energized.

After a few minutes of consideration, she decided to go back in. After all, there was much more to explore. Maybe the east side of the island wasn't as bad as the west. She didn't have her fingers crossed, but it was still worth a look.

The storm looked like it was a few hours out. The clouds were still nothing more than a thin grey line from where she was. It was maybe a *little* darker now. Unfortunately, it was definitely heading her way.

What a way to spend my first night home.

Oh well. She had to take the good with the bad. And there was still a chance of good to come. She turned the boat east and pressed forward.

After three hundred yards, she saw something black in the water. It was volley-ball shaped, with a tiny red bulb blinking at its top. She closed in and saw the number four written on it. A buoy. Uncle Lucas had said there were scientists doing research in the area, so common sense dictated it belonged to them. No way was she going to mess with it, so she continued onward for another hundred yards. She found a place to anchor, and after checking her equipment, she hit the water with a splash.

Immediately, she extended her speargun and checked her surroundings for sharks. So far, the water seemed as empty as before. The encounter may have been an adrenaline-fueled thrill-ride, which in hindsight made her feel like a Hollywood action hero, but it also reinforced that lingering desire for self-preservation.

However, that feeling lifted when she saw the flourishing beds of seaweed waving about below her. Around here, the ocean looked healthy. Vibrant even. The coral looked healthy, with no signs of whitening.

For the most part, at least. There was some coral further to the east that looked sickly. The staghorn coral nearby looked mostly healthy.

The landscape was like a miniature mountain range, traveling far into the ocean. There were even a few fish swimming about, though there certainly weren't as many as there should be. Still, it was enough to boost her spirits.

She swam north, gradually following the ocean floor into shallower waters. As she passed between two large seaweed beds, she shook as a flash of orange zipped by her. She whipped to her right, seeing the three Atlantic salmon darting to the west. Almost as soon as she identified them, they disappeared from view. She knew evasion when she saw it.

Sicilia faced the east and pointed her speargun. Her first instinct was another shark. She eyed the 'mountain range' in front of her. There was no torpedo shape moving about. Just a series of bumps along the ocean floor.

Had the rebreather not been in her mouth, she would've grinned, then chastised herself for being paranoid. She would wait until she was back on the boat to do that. For now, she decided she had done enough diving. At least she got to witness a little beauty.

She turned around, then whipped back again. *Did I see what I thought I saw?* In her peripheral vision, one of the mountains had moved. It was fast; a blur of motion. Whatever made it had vanished as soon as she redirected her eyes toward it.

Sicilia's defensive instincts kicked back into gear. Her speargun was now pointed forward with intention, her finger now resting over the trigger. There was no more movement. She wished she had taken a photo of the landscape, because she could swear one of those little bulges was not there anymore.

What the hell's going on? Am I insane?

For a few minutes, she held position. During that time, the water remained still. She tried to convince herself it was just a mirage caused by the sunlight and distance. Yet, she *knew* something had moved—and it was no shark. She was nervous, but also curious. Slowly, she swam ahead, keeping the weapon pointed straight ahead of her. Her eye was lined up along the shaft. All she needed to do was squeeze the trigger.

After thirty yards, she didn't see anything.

Probably nothing.

She let herself sink, still intently watching the east. When she landed, she felt something squishy. It wasn't like any coral or rock, and it definitely wasn't seaweed. It was like kneeling over a leathery sponge. A small black cloud formed around her.

Air bubbles burst from her mouth as she shrieked. She had landed on a rotting fish. It was white, its blank eye staring up at her. She walked along the seafloor, stepping on another one. When she turned, she saw another. Then another. There was a whole mass grave of dead fish lying about.

She kicked her legs, allowing herself to hover. After catching her breath, she realized there was a whole world of dead fish spread about. It was fascinating, yet terrifying. They were mostly tuna, their bluish color now white, almost like the dead coral she discovered on the other side of the island.

Most of them had died recently. The more decayed ones had been here longer, and were mostly different species. She recognized a few salmon, flounder, and some dead moray eels. The rest looked like tuna.

She backpedaled toward the shallows. That's when, in her peripheral vision, she spotted movement. Once again, it was for a split-second. This time, however, there was more evidence that something was there. Soot billowed from the seafloor where it ducked between some coral. She closed in. If it was a predator, her best bet was to stand her ground. She couldn't identify it, but she figured it had to be a shark. This did appear to be the direction that those salmon were fleeing from.

She glided a few more feet. She caught a glimpse of its bulk before she lost it behind another jagged piece of rock. She followed the slant with her eyes. There was more soot, as well as a few pieces of shredded seaweed. It was coming toward her. She elevated slowly.

The thing emerged.

Her heart skipped a beat. She fired the speargun. There was the sound of a metallic *clunk!*

Sicilia lowered the weapon and watched the 'predator' sink to a watery grave. Though it had a dorsal fin, it was no shark. In fact, it didn't use a caudal fin, but twin propellors. It was ray-shaped and bright white in color. Spiraling down alongside it were little glass fragments.

She had shot a drone.
Sicilia lowered her weapon, then her head.
Shit.

CHAPTER 7

When the screen went fuzzy and the controls unresponsive, Roy had gone into a minor tantrum, cussing out the stupid woman who shot down his drone. Brett, who was a little more laid back, wisely gave him five minutes to cool down before suggesting they take the boat over to her.

Roy stood at the forward deck, clutching the bow rail as he watched the hull slice through the water below. Something about the waves and the mist helped his mood. Still, the institution was not going to be pleased when they received the news. Already, he was dreading the next video conference. On the flipside, he was grateful that he wasn't diving in that area at that time. Otherwise, he'd probably have a spear run through his abdomen right now.

After a few moments, he pointed ten degrees off the port bow. "I see her boat."

Brett slowed the vessel then came out on deck. "At least she didn't run off."

"Probably trying to retrieve her spear," Roy said.

"Oh, be nice," Brett said.

"That was a five-thousand dollar piece of equipment. One that we *really* need," Roy said.

"Well, that's the risk we run when we go wandering in somebody else's backyard."

Roy was ready to continue arguing, but he couldn't deny his assistant's point. The guy was well on his way to earning his PhD and running his own research projects. He deserved it too. He was a smart guy and a good assistant, despite the quirk of not putting everything back where it belonged.

"Ah-ha! Over there," Brett said, pointing a few dozen yards ahead of the skiff. The water broke, and the diver appeared.

Brett hurried back into the pilothouse and brought the vessel nearer to hers.

Sicilia bit her lip when she heard the groan of a large boat engine behind her. It was obvious who it was, and she wasn't looking forward to the inevitable interaction. She continued swimming to the skiff, then placed her speargun and weight belt inside. Removing her goggles and rebreather, she turned around and smiled at the two men on the dock.

There was a brief look of surprise on the taller man's face. Maybe he wasn't expecting to see a woman, or maybe not a woman as beautiful as her. She preferred to think the latter. He couldn't have been much older than her. She pegged him at around thirty. Then she considered the fact that he was a doctor in marine biology. Considering the lengthy time to receive that education, let alone the time involved it would take to lead his own research project, he was probably around forty. If so, he had aged gracefully.

The other was a lot younger. Mid-twenties at the most. It was hard to peg that one as a scientist, judging by the comical *Star Trek* shirt he was wearing. Then there were the huge, rounded glasses. It was an odd sight that both made him look smart, and hilariously comical at once. Interestingly, he seemed more fixated on the taller man's reaction.

Figuring she'd start things off, she waved a hand at them, as though delighted to see them. "Hi!" To her relief, the taller scientist smiled and waved back. A good sign. Anything else would've expressed frustration.

"Hi. Hate to intrude on your little hunt…" he said.

"Any luck?" the other one said.

Now, Sicilia was smiling for real. These guys had her kind of humor. Might as well play along.

"Oh, you should've seen the whopper I just bagged down there! Had to be *this* big!" She held her hands about three feet apart. "Probably worth three grand on the mainland."

"Five, actually," the taller man said. Sicilia's smile faded somewhat.

"Damn. Price is going up these days," she replied. "For what it's worth, I'll let *you* have it for free."

"Probably not worth much at this point."

Finally, Sicilia broke character. "Look, I'm sorry. I thought it was a—something else. I should've waited a moment to identify the target before squeezing off a shot."

The taller man chuckled. "I'm just giving you a hard time."

The relief made Sicilia feel ten pounds lighter. "I've got more than enough money. I'll order you a new one. I'm Sicilia, by the way. You want me to call you *Doctor*?"

"Oh, he'd like that *very* much," the younger man said. It was intentionally barely audible, as was his chuckle.

The scientist shot him a glare, then turned back to Sicilia. "Glad to meet you, Sicilia. You can just call me Roy. This is Brett. And yes, he's as obnoxious as he looks."

"I resent that," Brett said.

"No you don't."

"Okay, maybe you're right."

Sicilia laughed. "With those glasses, I couldn't imagine otherwise." This time, Roy's laugh was genuine. Brett, meanwhile, displayed an exaggerated expression of shock.

"Damn!"

"I like her already," Roy said.

"Uh-huh," Brett said, nodding. *That's obvious as daylight. Ten minutes ago, you were referring to her as a stupid bitch.*

"So, where'd you come from? I thought only Mr. Instone lived on this island."

"Yeah. For us, you practically appeared out of thin air."

"For a while that was the truth," Sicilia replied. "I grew up here. Mr. Instone's my uncle. He picked me up and brought me back from Key Elliot."

"Oh, I see. Back for a visit?" Roy asked.

"No. For good, I think."

"Well, there are *two* houses," Brett said. Roy resisted the urge to roll his eyes.

"I know. I'm just making conversation," he whispered. "Plus, nobody was *in* that second house."

"Until now," Brett said. He didn't bother to keep his voice down.

"Hey, so what's going on around here?" Sicilia said. She sounded genuinely concerned.

Roy stammered. His first instinct was to curse Brett out, but didn't want to make a scene in front of the resident. *Damn it, you stupid idiot. She now thinks we're a couple of creeps.*

He cleared his throat. "I, uh...no-no-no! We just thought the other house was abandoned or was up for sale, or, uh..."

"What? No, I meant the research you're doing?" Sicilia said. Roy closed his eyes. Good thing there was a couple hundred feet between them because if they were any closer, she'd probably notice he was turning red. Brett noticed though, and it took everything not to break out in laughter.

"Oh, that. I don't know how much your uncle told you, but we've been detecting severe traces of dioxin in this area. We think there's a source nearby, but we can't seem to trace it."

"It's bizarre, actually," Brett said.

"How so?" Sicilia asked. She swam closer so she wouldn't have to shout.

"It's kind of hard to explain, but to put it simply, we've been testing the waters every day. To track the dioxin levels, we test the same areas repeatedly. Surface level and deeper waters," Roy said. "We've been detecting high traces, both in the water and the fish we've examined. But each day, the dioxin levels fluctuate."

"Fluctuate? How?" Sicilia asked.

"One day, we'll get severe levels on the north side of the island while getting lower readings on the south side. Then vice versa the next day, or maybe elevated levels of toxin on the east," Roy continued.

"Are these one at a time, or are there ever two or more spikes at once?" Sicilia asked.

Roy would've smiled had the subject matter not been so serious. This girl was a critical thinker. She seemed to have a handle on how data worked. Too bad she didn't pursue science. She'd make a good assistant. Definitely would enjoy her company more than *Spock* standing to his left.

Yeah, sure, that's what you're envisioning. Working in a lab with her. Riiiight. He wanted to tell his inner voice to shut up. Sometimes, it felt like there was a separate, judgmental, sarcastic son-of-a-bitch entity in his head.

"Just one at a time," he said.

"So, does that suggest that the source is…mobile?"

Roy nodded. "Like we've said, it's an odd scenario. I suppose you've seen the dead fish down below while you were—spearing my drone." He laughed to show he wasn't genuinely irritated. At least, not anymore.

Brett tucked his head down and pretended to cough. "I can think of some spearing *you'd* like to do."

"Brett, you mother—" Roy smiled. At least, that was the expression. "Hey, I almost forgot, there's the fish guts that need to be scrubbed off the stern deck."

"I can hose it off," Brett said.

"Nah. It's pretty caked. I don't see any method working other than a good ol' fashioned hand scrub."

Brett snorted. *Payback's a bitch. I gotta own it.* "Alright, I'll get a little *"Wax on, wax off"* action going." He bowed like a karate sensei and headed off to the rear of the ship.

Roy breathed a sigh of relief. When he looked back at Sicilia, she was chuckling. Now that she was closer, it was clear she'd heard everything said. He felt himself turning red again. This beautiful lady had a good sense of hearing. And she definitely was beautiful. Luckily, she seemed to have a good sense of humor as well.

Roy smiled. Up until five minutes ago, he was hating this assignment to the core. Now, he was hoping to stick around forever. *Hell, I wouldn't mind it if it took me six months to find the source of dioxin. Maybe the ocean is doing me a favor with these fluctuating spikes.*

"To answer your question, I did see the dead fish," Sicilia said.

"Beg your pardon..." He then realized he had asked her about the dead fish before his mind went into fantasy-land. "Oh! Right! Where was I going with that—Oh, yeah! You see, we examined that area yesterday and those fish weren't there. They died within the last twenty-four hours. Similar things have happened in other regions. I just can't make sense of it."

"Well, if I can be of any help, let me know. I love this place, and frankly, the fact that so much pollution is affecting it is breaking my heart. If I can make it stop, I'll be more than happy to lend a hand. Speaking of which, you gonna join me down here?"

Roy raised an eyebrow. *She wants me down for a swim?* His heart fluttered—doubly so when he saw her grin.

"You mean, in the water?"

"Yeah, duh," she said, laughing. "I figured you were planning on recovering your drone. I can help you with that."

It seemed feeling like a complete idiot was Roy Brinkman's thing today. Had it really been that long since he had been on a date? Let alone a date with someone this smoking beautiful? He'd been out working so much between the labs and the water that a personal life seemed impossible. He chastised himself mentally, reminding himself that this woman was a resident and he didn't want to make a fool of himself. Not too much, at least.

"Oh, you don't have to do that," he said. "I just need to go down, get a line on it, then haul it back up. It's not *that* heavy."

"I figured as much. I just didn't want to mess with it any more than I already had," Sicilia replied. "You sure you don't want me to replace it? I can have another one delivered with express shipping by tomorrow! I can get you a much better model. Hell, I've seen drones that can dive to nearly four thousand feet. Of course, they have to be operated by cable, but I can afford that too."

"Oh goodness, ma'am! That's not necessary. We've got insurance on this thing. I can blame it on a manufacturing error, and claim the damage was done by a reef or a shark or something. They won't look into it. Trust me."

"But aren't they just gonna give you another shitty one? That thing won't go down more than two-hundred feet. Yeah, it's wireless, which is cool, but you're still limited in the range in which you can explore. Shouldn't your organization have given you a submersible?"

Roy nodded, while resisting the urge to make a few comments about his overseers at the institution.

"Let's just say, based on all the observations you've made, that you'd probably make a better project manager than those in charge," he said.

"Ah. Taking orders from people who work in an office?"

Roy nodded. "Who haven't set foot out of Austin in fifteen years." He blew a heated sigh, then forced those idiots from his mind. "Give me a minute to get my rebreather and we'll go get that drone. You remember where it landed?"

"I'll lead the way," she said.

Roy strapped his rebreather back on and fixed his goggles. He ignored the crude gesture by Brett as he approached the diving deck, located behind the transom.

He hit the water with a splash and joined Sicilia, who fixed her rebreather and goggles. She waved him on to follow him, then dipped below the water. He summersaulted forward, then stroked. She was already almost twenty feet ahead of him. She swam with the grace of a bottlenose dolphin, waving both flippers like a fluke. She slowed, only to make sure he was behind her, then to check her bearings. She spotted the large slab of rock where the drone appeared.

In that moment, the tension reappeared. She remembered why she was on guard. The presence of the marine biologist and his vessel did little to alleviate that. Something had moved in the distance, and whatever it was, it was bigger than that drone.

Sicilia paused, eyeing the east once more. She could see that same 'empty' spot where that large boulder had been. She *knew* she saw it move.

She almost yelped when she felt Roy's hand tap her shoulder. Using her body language, she pretended she was just looking for the location, concluding with a fake 'ah-ha' moment when she pointed to the rocks. She led him to the bottom past the ledge, where the drone lay near a piece of staghorn coral. The drone had lodged itself pretty well, forcing them to carefully remove it without injuring themselves on the antlers. With the drone clutched in his arms, Roy gave a thumbs up, then started swimming toward the surface.

The boat was almost directly above them. Roy found that odd, considering they were right next to it when they dove, and he could've sworn they swam a little over a couple hundred feet east.

When he turned his gaze, he realized there were two shapes blocking the sunlight. Another vessel had come near his. It was a little smaller, maybe fifty-to-sixty feet in length. Lucas Instone, perhaps?

The two divers moved to the left, coming up on the stern of the *Europa*. As soon as they broke the surface, they could hear Brett on the radio. This time, his tone was one of frustration and anger.

"Yes!... Diamond Green, a little atoll twenty-miles northeast of Elliot Key... No, I'm not a resident! What does that matter?"

"What's going on?" Sicilia asked.

Roy looked to the other boat. When he saw the rusty paint, the skull flag waving from the crow's nest, and caught the stench of dead fish, he realized who it was. "Oh, great. Just what we need."

"Who is it?" she asked.

"It's the Glasses," he replied. He climbed aboard his vessel, then helped Sicilia up.

"The Glasses?"

"Dawn and Mel. I suppose, if you haven't been here for a long time, you probably don't know who they are."

Sicilia studied the filthy vessel. The fiberglass covering the steel hull was almost entirely exposed. There was hardly any paint left on the bow. There were sections of wood railing that were broken, as well as a cracked window on the pilothouse. Almost matching the appearance of their vessel were the Glasses. They almost resembled the homeless people she saw in Northern Ohio when doing a photoshoot. So much so, she almost expected to see cardboard signs reading "*Anything helps. God bless.*" But the looks on their faces weren't the self-pitying expressions of beggars. These people looked like they went to war every day. At least, in terms of their demeanor. Physically speaking, they in no way resembled warriors. The man had a large beer belly that jiggled with every move he made. It was so comical it was as though the guy had been plucked out of some kids' cartoon show. The wife, Dawn, wasn't much better. She was less heavy set, but her hair looked equally cartoonish as her husband's belly. It was as though she had been electrified, it was so frizzled. Both of them wore short sleeve shirts and overalls.

"No, I don't. But I have a feeling I've got a good read on them already." Sicilia's eyes went to the shark teeth that lined the pilothouse and gunwale of their vessel. One particular feature she found odd was the preserved snout of a sawfish that protruded over the bowsprit. *Poachers.*

"Don't know what they expect to find here," Roy muttered. He looked up at Brett, who was on the flybridge, tapping his leg while waiting for a reply from the Coast Guard. "What's going on?"

"Is that a serious question?" Brett said. "I spotted those idiots with my binoculars. They hooked a blue shark and severed its fins."

"You get it on film?"

Brett held up his smartphone. "Voila!"

"Yes! Nice work!" Roy said. It'd be a distant video, but hopefully enough to provide evidence to the authorities. Plus, he had the other dead specimen on his vessel to show them.

His mood soured when he saw the Glasses moving about on their ship. They looked like pirates about to conduct a raid. And, somehow, he had a feeling they were the type to do such a thing if it meant staying out of jail.

The husband, Mel, had a crooked grin on his face. He was missing a couple of front teeth, his hair was balding, and Roy could never get close enough to confirm, but it always looked like one eye was smaller than the other. He was uncoiling a rope, while Dawn disappeared below deck.

Roy's heart skipped a beat when she reemerged with a speargun. "Oh, this can't be happening."

"Now, how 'bout you consider minding your own business?"

There was a glint of metal at the end of the rope. As Roy feared, it was a triple-grip hook. These crazies were actually getting ready to storm their vessel.

Roy glanced back at the skiff, then at Sicilia. He felt guilty for having her aboard at the worst possible time. Unfortunately, he wouldn't be able to get her to her boat, or on land for that matter, in time. He didn't know the Glasses' history, but he'd had a couple of unpleasant run-ins before. None measured up to this.

"What's the status on the Coast Guard?" he asked Brett.

"At this rate, your guess is as good as mine."

It was a suitable answer for the Glasses. They throttled their vessel ahead then started circling around the front of the *Europa* with intent to line up with the portside bow rail.

Roy hurried to the winch and hauled the anchor in. The mechanical gears cranked, the chain rattling as it spun back into place.

"Come on! Come on!"

Sicilia was leaning over the port rail to see past the pilothouse. "They're turning around. They're coming in close."

The anchor came in. "Brett, punch it!"

The assistant darted into the pilothouse, engaged the throttle, and spun the helm to starboard, pointing them away from the Glasses. They could hear the cackling laughter from the two maniacs pursuing them.

All it took was a small turn to port for them to close in. Mel stood on the foredeck, rope in hand. He swung the hook like a lasso then let it fly. There was a loud *cling* as the hook struck the guardrail. The line went taut.

"Shit!" Roy exclaimed. He didn't have any firearms on hand...something that would change as soon as he got to the mainland. IF he ever made it back. Unfortunately, Sicilia had tossed her speargun into her skiff, rendering them without any projectiles to fight back with.

The Glasses secured their line to a winch and began reeling it in, keeping the line tight.

"We gave you a chance," Dawn shouted. Her voice matched her witch-like appearance.

"Oh, go fuck yourself!" Sicilia said. She drew her knife and ran it along the rope. After a few sawing motions, the line broke free, the tri-hook falling freely along the deck.

Without the fishing vessel in tow, the *Europa* doubled in speed almost instantly. They could hear the cursing of the fishermen behind them. Roy shook his head. No, they were no longer fishermen. They were pirates now as far as he was concerned.

The Glasses were inching closer, their vessel being a tad faster than the *Europa*. Roy stood at the transom, watching his pursuers. Dawn was at the helm, while the bastard Mel was fastening another tri-hook. There was a sick smirk on his face. He was *enjoying* this chase. And that was simply another red flag indicating these people were serious with their intent.

The biologist's eyes widened as he witnessed Mel place the hook down, then lift up his wife's speargun. He swung it over the bow and took aim.

Roy grabbed Sicilia by the arm and forced her to the deck. There was a hiss of air, like something from an angry snake, followed by a clang of metal. The spear hit the ladder bar leading up to the pilothouse.

Inside, Brett heard the *thud* reverberate through the deck. "Holy Jesus!"

Roy bared his teeth in anger. "Alright, enough's enough." He stood up and removed his scuba tank. "Mind helping me, Miss?"

Sicilia rose to her feet. Everything was happening so fast, it was surreal. For the past hour, she was worried about a threat being *under* the water. She never thought she'd be getting chased by a pair of married psychos!

"What can I do?"

"Hold on to this." Roy placed his scuba tank on the gunwale, facing the back end toward the incoming vessel. Sicilia held it in place while he grabbed the tri-hook. "Hold it loosely. Tilt it just a little upward…okay good. Be ready to let go…"

As he raised the hook like a hammer, she realized what he was going to do. She winced, anticipating the kick of a ruptured tank. Roy struck the valve, rupturing the burst disc. As soon as contact was made, the tank disappeared from the transom. They heard the shattering of glass and the angry scream of its female pilot.

They watched as Mel rushed into the pilothouse. The windshield was destroyed, the tank now clanging the inside of the boat as it whipped about for another few seconds. After it settled, Dawn reappeared, relatively unfazed save for a few glass cuts on her cheeks and arms.

The chase resumed.

"I think we pissed them off," Sicilia said.

"Those two were born pissed off," Roy said. "They're perfect for each other. They should live a nice long life together—in an insane asylum."

"What are we gonna do? They're still coming," she said.

Roy shrugged. "Keep fending them off I suppose. Hope you know how to throw a good punch, because if we can't deter them from boarding, then—"

Sicilia unfastened her scuba tank. "Personally, I'm getting quite the kick out of launching projectiles at them."

Roy chuckled. "Me too." The levity vanished as soon as he noticed Mel had loaded another speargun. For the second time, he forced Sicilia down. Again, the spear zipped overhead, this time shattering the cabin rear window.

Roy grimaced as the hundreds of shards pelted the deck. "Now, I'm *really* pissed."

They stood up and prepped the next scuba tank for launch.

"Hey, guys? What would you think about a little reinforcement?" Brett called out. Roy and Sicilia turned around, eager to see who they hoped to be the Coast Guard. Instead, it was not a cutter coming toward them from the east, but a sixty-foot fishing vessel.

To Sicilia, it was even better. She waved at Uncle Lucas' vessel. He was coming right for them.

"Mr. Instone," Roy said. "Must've picked up on our radio call."

As the vessel closed in, Sicilia saw the six-foot-three, muscular hero from her childhood standing on his flybridge. In his hand was a .30-06 rifle, aimed squarely at the Glass' vessel. There was a crack of gunfire and a thud of metallic impact. Then came the alarmed curses of two angry, but panicked fishermen. When Roy and Sicilia looked back, the Glasses turned to starboard and began retreating south.

For good measure, Uncle Lucas fired another round, striking the port quarter just below the gunwale. It was far above the waterline, nothing that would threaten them to sink. It was simply a much-needed "don't come back" warning.

Brett slowed the *Europa* to a stop, then joined the others outside as they caught their breath. Surprisingly, only now was Sicilia feeling the shakes. The chase itself was tense, but oddly exciting. Perhaps she was a more adventurous girl than she thought.

"Goddamn!" she shouted, raising her hand for a high-five. Roy grinned and completed the gesture, while Uncle Lucas steered his boat close.

With his rifle in hand, he stepped to his port side to greet them. "What did I say about language, young lady?!"

"Oh, Uncle," she said, chuckling. Lucas smiled.

"You guys alright?"

"Nothing we won't recover from," Roy said. He pointed at Sicilia. "I got to meet your niece."

"She's a pretty one, isn't she?" Lucas said. Roy nodded, unsure if it would come off as inappropriate to say 'hell yes'.

"Thanks for the save," Sicilia said.

"Seems I'm doing you all kinds of favors today," Lucas joked. "So, what happened here? I see the Glasses are still buzzing around like the horse flies they are."

"Long story short, Brett caught them finning sharks, tried calling the Coast Guard, and I guess they didn't like it," Roy said.

Lucas shook his head. "Good lord. I've seen those two get angry and belligerent, and I've heard of them getting into brawls, but never *this* hostile." He looked over at Sicilia. "What about you, kiddo? You alright?"

"Heck of a first day, that's for sure," Sicilia said.

"No kidding," Roy said.

"So, how'd you guys meet? I see you're both in your diving gear."

Sicilia grinned nervously, thinking about the true story. "Well, you can say we've had a little run in."

"We were diving in the same general area, got to know each other, and she decided to help me collect samples. Then those idiots showed up, and you know the rest," Roy said. He subtly winked at her. *No need for him to know about the drone situation.* Her barely-noticeable smile signaled her appreciation. At least, it was barely noticeable from a distance. Roy, however, couldn't miss it if he tried.

They could hear the echo of thunder in the distance. Lucas looked to the east. As though on cue, the wind picked up. It wasn't severe, but it was a sign of things to come.

"That'll keep those idiots away for now," Lucas said. "Probably a good idea for you guys to keep close to the island until it passes over."

"I was thinking the same thing," Roy said. "Well, sir, I appreciate you coming by and saving our behinds."

Sicilia cackled. "I see he's got you well-trained already."

"Actually, I was hoping to meet up with you, Doctor," Lucas said. "I was trawling about a half mile out, and I netted something I've never seen before. I was hoping you'd be willing to take a look at it."

"Oh!" Roy was genuinely surprised. "A fish?"

"I suppose you can call it that," Lucas said. "Though it's one ugly looking one. Not something I've ever seen around here in my fifty-eight years of life."

"Sure. Let's dock and see what you've brought me."

"Don't forget about my skiff," Sicilia said.

"Good thing we're not racing to the dock," Roy joked.

CHAPTER 8

"Holy fucking shit! Jesus Christ!" Roy exclaimed. Standing on the dock extending from Lucas Instone's property line, the marine biologist thought he was having a dream. What he was looking at couldn't be real. It wasn't possible.

For this specimen had been extinct for over three-hundred million years.

After several moments of silence, Roy lifted his gaze from the red-brown colored creature lying at his feet over to Lucas, who stood cross-armed, leaning back against the hull of his vessel.

Roy cleared his throat. "Pardon my French."

Had the scenario been any different, Sicilia would've been laughing hysterically. But, though not to the extent of Roy Brinkman, she too was quite interested at the dead creature.

"What is it?"

Roy was hesitant to answer. He looked to Brett. "Am I going insane?"

Brett shrugged his shoulders. "Just now? Or in general?" Roy groaned. *Even now, the knucklehead had to be a comedian.*

"Don't quit your day job," Roy replied. He leaned down by the specimen. It was a little over a foot long. Its mouth was bony, like a pair of slabs that would crush and grind prey. Its appearance almost looked amphibious, including particularly the design of its fins, which almost resembled legs. Its eyes were enormous, indicating that the creature had come from deep waters. There were three black dorsal fins running down its spine, looking like miniature sails found on the back of marlins. Its tail was significantly narrower than its head.

Now Lucas was intrigued. Before, he was simply curious. He lived on the water his whole life, and knew there were countless species of fish, and there was no way a single man would recognize every single one of them. He certainly didn't expect this expert to be flabbergasted.

"So... is it safe for me to assume this thing is rare?" Roy smiled. He was genuinely speechless. Lucas then looked to Brett. "Is he usually like this?"

Brett grinned. "No. I'm quite amused by it, actually."

"You would be too if you actually knew what we were looking at," Roy said.

Now, Lucas was borderline impatient. "*What* is it?!"

Roy took a deep breath. "I don't want to get ahead of myself, and I need to get in touch with other experts to confirm this—but I think we might be looking at a surviving member of the species *Materpiscis*."

Lucas pretended to gasp in amazement, then went back to a straight face. "And that is…?"

"Latin for Mother Fish. If I'm right, this little mama lived during the Devonian Age. Look at this!" He pointed at the little stringy object extending from its belly. "You see this? It's an umbilical cord."

"It's a baby?" Sicilia asked.

"No. Fossil records indicate remarkable preservation of the umbilical cord after birth. Sometimes, they'd still be connected to the mother for a period of time. It's really incredible."

"Son of a—" Lucas stopped himself, much to Sicilia's disappointment. Still, he looked like he was about to leap over the moon. "I found a gosh darn *dinosaur*! I'm gonna be rich and famous!"

"Well, unfortunately, I don't know about the rich part. Or the famous part, at least, not outside of the science community."

"Way to piss in his cornflakes," Sicilia said. Lucas shook his head in disapproval. It was obvious his niece was trolling him at this point.

"First thing's first: I gotta document this little guy right away," Roy said. "Sir, where did you find it?"

"Trawling off the Banker Reefs. A mile or so east of here," Lucas said.

"How deep?"

"It's relatively shallow there. Hundred yards, roughly."

"Was it dead when you brought it on board?" Brett asked.

"Dying," Lucas said. "Much like the forty-pounds of mackerel I caught. You guys really need to find what's poisoning these waters. I'm begging you at this point."

"I understand, Mr. Instone. Believe me, I'm trying my best with what I have," Roy said.

"I've told you before, you can call me Lucas. For what you're doing around here, and for saving Sicilia from the Glasses, you can consider me your friend."

Roy smiled. The statement genuinely warmed him. "I can't take all the credit. She played a big role in saving our—rear ends. Regarding the water, just bear with me. I'm gonna *try* and get in touch with my superiors. With a little luck, maybe I can get some better equipment."

"A *little* luck?" Brett said.

"Yeah." Roy nodded, defeatedly. "There's more important things to spend money on, like expensive meals and awards ceremonies for VPs who sit in an office all day." He knelt down by the specimen. "Who knows? Maybe we'll have one dedicated to us soon!"

"I want a cut of that," Lucas said.

"Deal," Roy joked. He picked the specimen up and took it to his vessel, while Brett collected the container of dead mackerel.

"How come I have to do all the heavy lifting?"

"Because you're my bitch," Roy joked. Sicilia cracked up laughing at that.

"Behave, boys," Lucas said.

"Yes, Dad," Roy joked. He smiled. Only known the man for a few days, and they were already bantering like they'd known each other for years. "Hey, you alright if we remain docked here for the duration of the storm?"

Lucas examined the approaching clouds, then looked over his right shoulder. He couldn't see Diamond Cove from where he stood due to the elevation in the center of the peninsula, but knowing the island like the back of his hand, he was able to make his determination.

"Actually, if Sicilia is alright with it, it might actually be better to dock on her side. The peninsula should help block some of the waves from battering your boat too much. Would probably suck to do your lab work while trying to remain upright."

"I'm good with it," she replied. "You can take my skiff there along the way."

"Will do," Roy said. "I appreciate it. Come on, Brett. Let's get this bad boy started." He entered the pilothouse, started the engine, and took the *Europa* around the peninsula, leaving Sicilia and Lucas standing together on his beach.

Sicilia felt lost in a dream as she watched the vessel disappear around the edge of the southern shore. She should have been jittering with anxiety, considering they were literally just chased by a pair of murderous fishermen. Instead, she felt energized. Her spirit was rejuvenated, and it was like nothing she had ever experienced. As a child, and as a lonely wife who realized she wasn't appreciated, she had read and watched countless stories of adventure. She was aware it was fiction and not real life, and that two people couldn't fall in love so quickly. But she couldn't deny that this felt like one of those make-believe adventures. She couldn't help but suspect that it would not feel as such had it not been shared with Roy.

"Hey, kid?"

Uncle Lucas' voice seemed like it was coming from across the island, even though he was standing a couple of feet away from her. Sicilia whipped around. "Oh, sorry. What's up?"

"I thought I was gonna have to throw water in your face to get your attention there," he said.

"Sorry. I guess I was lost in la-la-land for a moment."

Lucas glanced in the direction of Roy's vessel. *Oh, boy. That didn't take long.*

They could hear the thunder rolling in the distance. Sicilia sneered at the weather, as though it was deliberately tampering with her first night back home. She was looking forward to sitting on the beach late at night, maybe getting lost in a book, or even simply watching the gentle waves while the sun set.

"I suppose I oughta head in before we get rained on."

"Ha! Give me a break. We still got plenty of time and daylight," Lucas said.

"For what?" she asked.

Lucas shook his head with scorn. "'For what?'" He walked up the beach, picked up his volleyball, and tossed it at her. Sicilia caught it, though mostly with her chest. "Let's see if you still have your reflexes, kiddo."

Sicilia laughed. "Alright, old man. Let's see if you still have *your* reflexes."

"Oh! Old man, ay? I see how it is!"

"Volley for serve?"

"Nah. I'll let you have it. Something tells me I'll be getting the ball back shortly."

"Have it your way," Sicilia said. "Zero-zero…"

CHAPTER 9

"Son of a—" Sicilia stopped, not because of her uncle's strict policy on profanity, but to spit out the sand in her mouth. She rested on her hands and knees, watching the volleyball settle in the sand a couple of feet away. She should've had it. There was no excuse. She saw the way Lucas' hand moved. It was clear he was going for a slam-dunk over the net. Yet, she didn't counter in time.

"Oh! How about that!" Lucas hollered victoriously. "Twenty-to-eight! Who's the old man now?!"

Sicilia smirked. He was enjoying himself a little too much. Was this the reason he wanted her back on the island? To have someone to school in volleyball? The thought made her laugh.

She stood up and passed the ball over to him. "Yeah-yeah. Not over yet, Gramps."

"Looks like someone's relying on the naïve hope that she'll get on her game and turn around a twelve-point lead," he said.

"I've seen stranger things," Sicilia replied.

"Yeah? Like what?"

"Like you dancing to disco."

"Oh…you remember that?!"

"Uh-huh! How could I forget?"

Lucas bumped the ball against his own forehead in shame. "I grew up in the seventies. What do you expect? I can't believe you remember seeing that. You were only like six."

"Ha!" Sicilia took great joy in her childhood memory of walking to her uncle's front porch one evening and finding him dancing to *Bee Gees* in his living room. "Some things are just burned into your mind."

"Well, in that case, I'll do the same when I see your look of defeat," Lucas said. He struck the ball, sending it toward her. Sicilia knocked it back. For a good thirty seconds, they volleyed it back and forth.

It was coming back at her now. It was going far, but not quite out of bounds. She backtracked, made it in time, and knocked it back. For a second, it looked perfect. It was barely clearing the net, ready to hit the sand less than a foot past it. Except it never touched the sand. Uncle Lucas dove and clubbed it with his fists, sending it straight up. Sicilia didn't notice the slight mid-air arch until it was coming down on her side.

"Crap!" She ran for it, but it was too late. The ball struck down, launching a cloud of sand around it.

Lucas held his arms to the side. "Ha! Twenty-one to eight! I might have the miles on me, but I'd say it's the youngling who moved like a senior citizen today."

Sicilia stuck her tongue out at him. "Yeah-yeah, have your moment of glory."

"Believe me, I am." After whooping a couple more times, he walked to her side of the net. "You always were a sore loser."

"I think you're talking about yourself," she said.

He shrugged. "There's a small possibility of that."

"Small?! I remember kicking your butt when I was ten one morning, and you spent the whole rest of the day begging for a rematch."

"It wasn't simply because I lost. It was *how* I lost. I was off my game that day and I wanted to redeem myself."

Sicilia squeezed her eyes shut and shook her head. "Gotta restore that volleyball honor."

"That's right," he joked. "I'm surprised you're not feeling the same way, considering how off your game you were today."

"Out of practice," Sicilia said.

"Mmm, maybe. But I think your mind's elsewhere," Lucas said.

"Well, I *did* get chased by a couple of crazies today," she said.

"Nice try, but I don't think that's it," Lucas said.

"What? You think it's every day I encounter people who shoot spearguns at me and try to board my boat?"

"No, but again, nice try. I saw your face. You were exhilarated. Deep down, you're still that little adventurous kid who couldn't wait to go out and travel everywhere."

Damn. Even after ten years away, he still knows me too well.

"What if I said I was attacked by a shark?" she said.

"I'd say you look like you came out of it in one piece," Lucas said. Sicilia laughed, but only she knew he didn't realize she was being sarcastic. "I know *exactly* what it is," Lucas continued. "You're not thinking about something, rather some*one*."

"What?! No!"

Lucas danced side-to-side, snapping his fingers. "Sicilia's got a cruuuussssh!"

"Don't be ridiculous. I'm recently divorced—"

"And rebounding like a teenager," Lucas said. "I know who it was that infiltrated your mind, making it so easy for me to best you. You're thinking of our scientist friend."

"Don't be silly. I literally just met him," Sicilia said.

"Yeah? So?"

"I—" she struggled to think of some other excuse. "So, we had an interesting encounter."

"That's the best way it starts," Lucas said.

"You're acting like it's love at first sight."

"It was with me and your Aunt Mary," Lucas said. "I remember seeing her on the pier in Santa Monica. Told your dad who was with me at the time that I was gonna marry her. He told me I was foolish. Proved him wrong, didn't I?"

"Yes, you certainly did," she said. The soft way in which she spoke also served as an admission to her feelings toward Roy Brinkman. "He did save my life today."

"You might've saved his as well. He mentioned how you cut the rope," Lucas said. "Listen, kid. God has a plan for you. For whatever reason, He called for you to come home at this time. Maybe it has something to do with the doc. I don't know, I don't always pretend to know what God's plans are. But I do know He *does* have a plan for you."

Sicilia smiled. She wasn't completely certain of how religious she was, but it was obvious she wasn't nearly as dedicated as her uncle. She wasn't sure how to respond, so she decided to deviate from the subject.

"You think the Coast Guard will actually hunt down those freaks?"

"Hard to say. It's a big ocean, and with a storm on the way, they're probably fixated on other things right now," he said.

"But let's not get off topic. That Doctor Roy guy, he seems like a good fellow to me."

"We barely know him."

"I know enough," Lucas said.

"He swears!"

Lucas laughed. "Not everyone's perfect."

"He's only been here a few days. Probably won't be here many more."

"Then you have a limited time to make a memorable impression. Then, he might come back. And NO, I'm not talking about anything crude!"

"Yeeeesss, Uncle! I figured as much. You're as pure as sunshine, after all."

"I wouldn't go *that* far," Lucas said. "Invite him to your place for dinner tonight. See how it goes."

Sicilia raised her eyebrows. "You're serious, aren't you?"

"Can't pretend you're a little girl forever. Believe me, I've tried," he said.

"Still, it's my first night home. I figured you'd want me over for dinner."

"Always, but I'll have a hundred more chances. You have a limited time with the doc," he said. He pointed to her face. "Ah-ha! I see that sparkle in your eye."

"It's just the sand from me trying to catch the ball," she said.

"Right, sure. You're about as good of a liar as your dad was," he said. He gave her a hug. Right then, the thunder rumbled in the horizon. The sky was gradually darkening. Those clouds were no longer a thin grey line, but rather a black splotch, gradually rolling west. The wind was picking up speed. The pressure was starting to drop, almost making Sicilia's ears pop.

Lucas tapped her on the shoulder. "Get going, kid. I'll see you tomorrow."

"You sure you don't need help with anything here?"

"Nah, I got it. You go on. Good game, though."

"Ha! And you say *I'm* the poor liar!" Sicilia said. She gave him another hug then trotted over the hill to the other side of the peninsula. The wind was pushing her along as she went down the other side. The thunder was sounding like the roars of approaching beasts, hungry to feast on anything in their way.

It would be an hour at best before the first wave of misery would hit. Hopefully, Sicilia would have the house ready by then. She glanced at the dock as she approached her house. The *Europa* was docked opposite of her dad's fishing vessel. She could see lights on in the cabin. No doubt, Roy was busy doing some science work.

Good. She wasn't ready to invite him in yet anyway.

CHAPTER 10

The hour had struck six when the rain started coming down. Sicilia looked out the window to see a blackened sky. Trees were leaning to the west, their leaves threatening to shoot across the island. She could still see the *Europa,* though mostly due to the interior lights shining through the window. She hoped they managed to cover up that broken window in the rear of the cabin. But more importantly, she hoped that Roy Brinkman wasn't too busy.

The stir fry was almost done. The pork was smelling delicious, especially combined with the aroma of the carrots, onions, and peppers. She had red and white wine set out, though she wasn't sure if Roy even enjoyed alcohol. She was getting the butterflies in her stomach, but in a good way. This would be her first date since Bill.

Would it be considered a date? Dates are arranged, right? That's what makes them 'dates.'

Sicilia knew it was her jittery nerves that caused her to overthink this. Then again, there was no denying that her interest in Roy would not go unnoticed, especially when she presented the invoice for the drone she just ordered. It was top of the line, so much so, that she would undoubtedly receive a flabbergasted response. She mentally prepared herself to quickly shoot down any efforts to pay her back. As long as she wasn't making these kinds of purchases on a repeated basis, Sicilia had the money to spend.

Still, there was the slight worry that she was coming on too quick.

"Fuck it. I'm a free, independent woman. I want something, and goddamn it, I'm gonna fucking go after it." Even knowing her uncle wasn't nearby, she still found herself looking around for him. "Bastard's got me well trained already. He's probably in that house of his, putting a pillow over his head while chastising himself for putting me up to this." She chuckled at the thought. Uncle Lucas was a devoted Christian if she ever saw one. No such thing as sex outside of marriage. In fairness, he practiced what he preached. Also, though he was outspoken, he understood how the rest of the world worked.

Oh, Uncle. I'm not planning to take it THAT far. It's just dinner and a drink. As she thought this, she was lighting candles. A candlelit dinner…in the evening…

The self-awareness started creeping in.

Then again, I'm not saying I wouldn't MIND it if it went that far…

"Jesus, I've lived alone in this house for less than twelve hours and I'm already going stir crazy."

She finished cooking the stir fry, scooped it onto a serving dish, then arranged the dining room table. She printed the invoice then stepped toward the door. Since she started cooking and cleaning, she had been mentally rehearsing the way she'd ask Roy to join her. Up until thirty-seconds ago, she figured she had her approach down pat.

All of a sudden, she was lost. Everything she planned to say suddenly seemed wrong. Worse yet, there was another issue. That Brett guy. Her thoughts had been so focused on Roy, that she nearly forgot his assistant existed. Blatantly inviting one without the other would be awkward. Then again, so would the intended date with a third party involved.

She could afford to wait. The food was hot and ready, but wouldn't stay that way for too long. The time to figure something out was now. And chickening out was not Sicilia's nature, no matter how nervous she got. That observation brought a new sense of strength. She was nervous, and that only happened when she was pursuing *good* things. There were no butterflies with Bill. Maybe some chemistry, laughs, and even some excitement in the early days, but no nervousness. This was different. Something in her mind told her that was a good thing.

Either this would work out, or it wouldn't. Only one way to find out.

Sicilia grabbed a jacket, then tucked her chin down as she stepped outside. Already, the wind was assaulting her. Just another reason to move faster. She ran down the hill and onto the dock.

****

Brett shook his head as he watched the lightning flashing outside. "Damn. Stupid wind. I've lost the readings from Buoy Eight." Roy didn't bother to lift his eyes from the microscope. Brett suspected the doc didn't even hear him speak. Roy adjusted the tissue sample from the believed-to-be *Materpiscis.* To his right were blood samples taken from it, as well as other labeled samples taken from the mackerel given to them by Lucas. Up on the wall were several photos of the specimen in question, along with an x-ray image.

Roy finally lifted his head from the microscope. "There's dioxin in the tissue as well. Probably excreting it through the amphibious-like skin."

"So...you think this thing is a prehistoric species?" Brett said.

"I wanna say yes, but I'm trying not to get too far ahead of myself. If I called Doctor Bain right now and explained what we were looking at, he'd probably cut this operation off at the knees."

"So, this was an ocean fish?" Brett said.

Roy stared at him. "Well...we *found* it in the ocean. Some PhD candidate you are."

"I mean...not an ocean fish, but a western species? Where did it swim during the Devonian Age?"

"If memory serves, it used to reside in the waters near where Australia is now," Roy said.

"What's it doing on this side of the globe?"

"It's been a long time since we thought they died out. I think it's safe to assume some of these species, or subspecies, may have migrated across the oceans in the millions of years leading up to now. Keep in mind, there's been massive continental shifts, which could've played a role. But it's not just a matter of distance..."

"But of depth," Brett said, completing the Doctor's thought. "Those eyes—those aren't like those what we found in the fossil record."

"No. I think it's an evolution. I think these species learned to live deep over the course of time. I think we simply haven't discovered one up until now," Roy said. "Before we can go further, I'll have to go over the records of all known species and compare the biology to our specimen here. One thing I *do* know, is that wherever this thing came from, it was LOADED with dioxin. So much so, I'm surprised the bastard isn't green."

A loud *ding* filled the room. An excited Brett hurried into the passageway and made his way to the kitchen. There was the sound of an opening microwave, followed by the aroma of preservatives of sodium-filled pizza sauce. There was a squirt of something, which was undoubtedly ranch dressing. A very hungry Brett Rollins stepped back into the passageway, yelping after nibbling on a freshly microwaved nugget.

"Oh, for heaven sake," Roy muttered. The nerd he mentored was more excited about his *pizza bites* than the possible discovery of a three-hundred-MILLION-year-old species. "How can you eat that crap?"

"It's good," Brett said. With a look of disgust, Roy turned away.

"I still have faith in you. I think once you hit thirty, you'll actually wanna eat *food.*"

"What? This *is* food."

"Oh, God give me strength," Roy said. "*This* is what higher education has brought us."

"I'm a marine biologist. Not a nutritionist. And we're on a budget. Had to pack cheap stuff in order to have enough to even eat on this trip. Unless you'd rather go fishing…"

This time, Roy's disgust was genuine. "This is my reality, where the best thing on this ship to eat is…" He leaned in toward Brett's plate. Some of the cheese, while oozing out of the so-called crust, still didn't even look fully melted… "this shit!"

There was a knock on the door.

"Who the hell?" There were only two people it could possibly be. Roy moved up the steps to the rear entrance. He opened the door and found Sicilia standing in a world of rain. "Oh! Ms. Instone! Come in out of the rain." She quickly did so.

"Hi. Hope I'm not bothering you."

"I'm sure you can't do anything I've had to endure from *this* guy," he replied, pointing at Brett and his pizza bites.

The assistant waved from the bottom of the stairway. "Hi Sicilia." She waved back. "You hungry?"

Sicilia forced a grin. "Uh, no thanks… well, yes actually…"

"Okay! I can microwave another plate—"

"On second thought..."

Roy shooed Brett away like an unruly pet. "Go watch one of your shows on your tablet."

"Fine. More for me," Brett joked. He vanished into the passageway.

Roy faced Sicilia. "Sorry about him. He's a brilliant mind on the subject matter of aquatics. Anything real life, well..."

"He's alright," Sicilia said.

"So, what can I do for you?"

Sicilia fought against her shyness. "Well, it looks like you've already eaten."

"Not yet," Roy said. "For better or worse. Unfortunately, our supply doesn't contain much that's better than what you've observed."

"Well, in that case, I'm here to the rescue," Sicilia said. Roy's eyes brightened. "You like stir fry? Pork flavored, pan roasted?"

"You serious?"

"Yeah. I got the table set up inside."

Roy tilted his head, trying to get a read on her without asking any embarrassing questions. Yet, he couldn't help himself on one: "Does this invite include Mr. Rollins?"

She smiled. "Let's just say he looks like he's happy with his microwaved shit."

She hates cheapo food. Woman after my heart.

"In that case, I'm not wasting any more time. Let me grab my jacket. Is there anything you'd like me to contribute?"

She giggled. "No, that's okay."

"Good, because all I have are canned goods, store-brand soda, and other stuff that probably wouldn't go with stir fry. Be right back." Roy hurried into the passageway into his quarters. He grabbed his coat and hurried back, passing Brett's cabin along the way. The jerk heard every word spoken between them and was looking at Roy with raised eyebrows and a shit-eating grin.

Fitting expression, considering the crap he's eating.

"I'll be out."

"And in," Brett muttered.

"Jesus, you—" Shaking his head, he allowed himself a quiet laugh and hurried back to the exit, where Sicilia awaited. She was more at ease now.

"Get ready to run. It's coming down pretty hard out there."

"After you," he replied.

They sprinted onto the deck and disembarked, then ran up the hill like a pair of children daring 'last one to the house is a rotten egg.' As soon as he was under a roof, Roy looked back at the water. Being able to eat real food on solid ground, while Brett rocked back and forth in that boat, made him *really* appreciate the offer. And the aroma was fantastic.

Roy hung his coat on a nearby hook, then stepped into the dining room.

"Oh, wow. Definitely better than that so-called pizza crap Brett packed."

"I'm glad I could rescue you," Sicilia said. Roy picked up one of the wine bottles.

"Gosh, Chateau Pape Clement. You're *really* going all out. Haven't drunk wine this expensive since I completed my PhD. And that was only because other people paid for it."

"It's the least I could do," Sicilia said. "After all, I did break your drone. Speaking of which—"

"Oh, don't worry about that. It was an accident," Roy said. "I'm sure I'll be able to get it replaced relatively soon."

"Go ahead if you like, but my solution's faster. And frankly, it helps you out a little more." Sicilia handed him the printout of the invoice and an image of the underwater drone she'd ordered.

Roy gazed at the image and specifications. "Uh…wait a minute…" Sicilia pulled his chair out for him. Good thing too. He needed to sit. "Holy—"

"You can speak freely. My uncle isn't here."

"Holy shit! Sicilia, you don't have to do this. This thing is freaking *expensive*!"

"Too late. Already ordered." She sat across from him and filled her wine glass. "I told you I'd replace the thing."

Roy stammered. For the first time in many years, he had been overwhelmed with gratitude. "You didn't—I don't know—I—uh—that was five grand. THIS is over thirty. More, actually, if you count all the freaking accessories you added. Four-thousand-foot tether?! GoPro HD camera. Scanning sonar.

Sensors. Manipulator arm." He leaned in closely at the paper. His jaw dropped. "Overnight shipping?!"

"Should be here by noon tomorrow," Sicilia said proudly. "They have an office in Miami. There're a few researchers along the Keys who order from them, so they developed their own delivery service as opposed to using *Fed Ex*. I gave them a call, made sure they have everything in stock. I offered a few extra bucks to persuade them to send a boat out in the morning."

Roy put the paper down and leaned back in his seat. "Jesus, you'd think you were trying to win my heart over." Sicilia sipped her wine. "How can you even afford this?"

She laughed. "I live on a private island."

"Nice try," he said. "Your uncle spilled the beans on the fact that the island has been in the family for generations. For anyone else, it'd cost a pretty penny. For you guys, aside from maintenance, I imagine it's mostly paid off. Unless you came from wealthy inheritance."

"I wish," she said. "No, my great-great-great-grandfather settled here long ago. Literally built this house and we've been living in it since. Obviously, there's been heavy work done over the century-and-a-half. But, that's not to say I haven't done well for myself. I've been on the go, doing advertising for a major company. To sum it up, I lived a pretty pampered life, with most of my expenses paid for in addition to having a pretty nice paycheck." *And a divorce settlement.*

"Gosh! So, you're implying this is a dime dropped in a pond for you," Roy said, holding up the drone invoice.

"I'm not SUPER rich, but I'm able to make a big purchase here-and-there," she replied. "Listen, I want you to have it, both for your research, and as gratitude for helping us figure out what's going on around here with the island. I didn't expect to come back to dying reefs and a dwindling fish population. That's not what I signed up for. So, this is my way of helping."

Roy was extremely grateful to hear her say that, and for reasons he would not say out loud. A woman in her early-thirties, living alone in a decent-sized house away from civilization, serving him expensive wine and providing him with a forty-thousand dollar piece of equipment that he in no way could afford...for a moment, it raised a red flag. Was this a desperate attempt to get his attention? That in itself wasn't the issue, but the extent she seemed to be going to would have been. Drastic measures such as this indicated that the person doing them would be clingy and extremely possessive, making it a risky business pursuing any further relationship.

Instead, however, he learned she had integrity. She cared for the sea and the health of the island, and was willing to help in any way she could to see it restored. Already, she provided him better assistance than the head of his department had in the last year.

"This will really help. We can search the deeper trenches around here," he said. "If there's a spill near this island, it'll likely be in deeper waters. And I highly suspect that, because that specimen your uncle brought me, it's loaded with the stuff. And I'm one-hundred percent positive it was living in deeper regions."

"You really think it's prehistoric?"

"I'm certain, but it takes work to confirm," Roy replied.

"Is it possible that if it was living in deeper waters where it could easily hide, you think that dumping of toxic waste could have driven it out?"

"That's—" Roy thought about it for a moment, "—very possible." He was so fixated over the animal itself that he hadn't yet considered that possibility.

"If something like that existed, and was driven out, I wonder what else was hiding in the deep," Sicilia said. "Maybe more sea creatures are about to be revealed."

"That would be something," he said. He filled his wine glass. Sicilia extended hers to make a toast.

"To saving our ocean…and new discoveries, and the fame and fortune they bring."

He chuckled, then touched his glass to hers. "Unfortunately, fame in the science community doesn't bring much fortune."

"Fortune doesn't just come in money," she said. Roy thought of her determination to solve the pollution issue.

"No, it does not," he said. They drank in unison, then commenced to eating and learning about each other. Meanwhile, in the back of Roy's mind, the thought lingered.

What else might have been driven up from the depths?

CHAPTER 11

Lucas stepped outside, getting a quick glance at the last rays of sunlight that beamed in from the west. They had turned grey from the cloud cover, and were quickly dwindling as the thick sheet of black rolled in from the east. Lightning streamed across the sky in thin, jagged formations.

He had been through countless storms in his lifetime. Still, like the rest of his species, Lucas was a creature of habit. He couldn't believe he had forgotten to take down the volleyball net. He had gotten caught up in his usual routine boarding up the boat windows as well as the second windows on the house, which were more susceptible to debris from the nearby trees. The net, which had only been put up recently for the first time in almost ten years, vanished from his mind. Now, he was stuck doing it in the wind and rain.

The droplets were like bee stings, zapping him all over. He flung his hood over his brow, tucked his head down, and began removing the stakes. At least the ground was moistened, which made it easier to get them out. He didn't worry about making the net look pretty. As long as it was rolled up and secured in the shed, he was fine. All he wanted to do was go inside, relax, and watch television.

With the net rolled up with its posts, he raced to the shed and tossed it in. The wind threatened to carry the door away, forcing him to tug with both hands to lock it shut. When he turned around, he saw a roaring sea lapping at his shore. He'd been through worse. Still, it was an eerie sight. It was a seemingly infinite stretch of pure power, which just a couple of hours ago, had been calm. Even now, the sky was continuing to darken. Within the next half hour, he would barely be able to see the shoreline from his living room window. But that was no problem, as he had no intention of doing anything else other than sitting on his chair with his feet up, and getting lost in a movie from his childhood. With the way the electrical system on the island functioned, he didn't have to worry about downed power lines like most people on the mainland.

Lucas hustled around the front of the house. The lightning flashed as he turned the corner, illuminating the entire shore. His eyes went straight to the peninsula. He froze. Something had rolled up onto shore. That side of the peninsula was mainly sand, not rocks like the Diamond Cove side.

"What the—?" Curiosity got the better of him. He wanted to know what he was looking at. He'd seen seals accumulate on the island before, but this was a big one. It was the right time of year, after all. With the world around him quickly darkening, he hurried into the house to grab a flashlight, then fought against the storm onto the southeast peninsula.

The closer he got, the larger he realized the thing was. It was definitely no elephant seal. It was about fifteen feet in length. He saw a flipper or a fin sticking high into the air. The way it was waving, definitely a flipper. He saw the big block of bulk that was its head.

Lucas realized he was looking at a small sperm whale.

"My heavens!"

He studied the specimen with his light. There were several obvious wounds in its hide, as though strips of flesh had been ripped away before it washed up. It was twenty-feet in length, maybe a year old. But undoubtedly a sperm whale, likely pushed up on shore by the storm.

Lucas immediately resented the existence of the storm, as well as his awareness of Sicilia's plans, as he had a hundred questions for Roy. What kind of injuries were these? Granted, it was safe to assume other creatures had taken bites out of it while the corpse was adrift. But it still didn't explain the other markings. There were rounded marks on its head and tail. He had been on the water all of his life, and the closest thing he ever saw on those were on mature adults after a deep sea hunt for food. The large, open wounds...most of them didn't even resemble bites from sharks or other organisms. It was almost as though a buzzsaw had cut into the poor creature. And where was the mother?

Lucas did a double-take when his light touched the fluke. The right side was facing up, almost making the mammal look like a shark. Then he noticed the wrinkles in the flesh at the center of the body. This twenty-foot sperm whale was literally twisted. Its *spine* had to be broken, judging by the disproportionate positions of the head and tail. A whale with a broken backbone? He'd never heard of such a thing.

The thing rocked as more swells pushed against it.

Lucas shook his head. "Heavenly Father, you are the Lord of all creation. And you *create* the strangest of mysteries." The thunder cracked loudly, as though responding directly. The rain intensified, as did the wind. A large swell broke against the rocks, spraying him.

Lucas spat. "Alright, Lord. I get it. I'm going back inside. I'll ask questions tomorrow." He could not wait to get them answered. This was one of the strangest things he had ever seen. One thing he did know; this was not a result of toxic waste.

In the meantime, however, he would put it from his mind. He had a bottle of wine and a comfy chair waiting for him inside. First, he needed a dry towel.

CHAPTER 12

"Wait-wait, hold on," Sicilia said, barely getting her words through the alcohol-induced laughter. They were in the living room, sitting on each side of the three-cushion couch. "You're seriously saying you don't have a place of address?"

"I'm serious," Roy said, halfway through his third glass of wine. At least, he was pretty sure it was his third. He was having so much fun with the banter, it might've been his fourth.

"No apartment? No house?" Sicilia continued.

"No. I'm always on the go," he said.

"Not even a box under a bridge?" she said, laughing at her own joke.

"You know, I tried, but got turned down by the bank," Roy said. "I use my parents' house for a mailing address. I'm just on the go so much that there's no point in wasting my paycheck on utilities and rent."

"That's smart—par for the course for a PhD, I suppose."

"Not sure about that. I've worked with many who couldn't find their way out of a paper bag," he said.

"Yeah? Give me an example?"

Roy briefly debated following through. He usually made a policy never to badmouth his associates. His mood and the alcohol easily defeated those barriers.

"Doctor Samuel Griss," he replied. "We went on a diving mission in Antarctica…"

"Antarctica?"

"Yes   ma'am!"

"My God, you really have been everywhere," she said.

"Pacific Ocean. Lower Indian Ocean, African coast. Did a little studying on an atoll in the east Atlantic, tracking the lunar effect on the growth rate on local birds—this is actually the project that involved Dr. Griss."

"The lunar effect affects their growth rate?" Sicilia asked.

"The babies, and probably not directly. The parents go out to sea to collect food and bring it back. They're nocturnal creatures, so they go out to hunt at night and feed the chicks in the morning. Griss and I would weigh them during the day. On nights where there is less moonlight, especially on a new moon, we'd find little to no increase in the offspring's weight. I believe it's because it's darker, thus the parents can't successfully catch as much food."

"That's fascinating. I never thought such experiments were done. I always thought it was all diving with dolphins and sharks," Sicilia said.

"So did Griss. The bastard was bored out of his mind. That actually goes into the story of why the asshole was so stupid: So, we're barbequing one night at the house on the atoll. Nothing major, just brats and so forth with the guys who work on the island. There's always a couple of men on site, there to essentially keep watch of the place; get rotated out every three months. Anyways, I'm chitchatting with them. It's just casual conversation, until someone points out that there's a boat in the distance. Nothing unusual, boats come around all the time, bringing people to view the islands and everything. In this case, however, we hear gagging in the background. It's *loud*, enough to make all four of us be like "what the hell?" And by the looks of it, it's got the attention of everyone on board, who's gathering around somebody.

"We couldn't make out what the chatter was, but it seemed that a lot of the tourists were pissed off at something. Or, as it turned out, someone. So, long story short, we decide to take a boat over there to make sure everything was alright. Turns out, they were there to shark watch, and apparently one of the experts was sick to his stomach. Like *really* sick—I honestly don't know what he was thinking getting on that boat to begin with."

"Money," Sicilia said.

"There's that," Roy said. "Anyway, the staff were dealing with the crowd on the boat. I guess the biologist on board was supposed to dive in a cage and hand fish to the sharks in the area. So, Griss, in a pathetic attempt to impress the ladies on the boat, raises his hand and states that *he* would do it. The staff initially said no, but then changed their minds, as this conversation was taking place in front of these tourists...all of which paid a hundred-something-dollars to see this. So, Griss and I get our dive gear, goes down into the cage, and the staff starts chumming for sharks."

"You went with him?"

"Hell yeah, I'm not gonna say no to diving with sharks," he said.

"Oh yeah? Nothing to do with the pretty babes on the boat?"

Roy shrugged. "I'm a guy, but I'm also a realist. What was I gonna do? Ride back to the mainland, or have one of them stay in my room on the island? Not likely. Anyway, I lost where I was—okay, so we were in the cage. There's a few sharks, but they're not coming close. We try to wiggle the tuna to create vibrations, but the sharks just aren't taking the bait. We couldn't communicate because of the rebreathers, but we both knew it was because the staff was over-chumming the water. Just too much scent, as well as vibration from the stuff breaking the surface.

"So, I get this fabulous idea…" Roy extended his arm and rolled back his sleeve to reveal a small scar below his wrist. "I decide to take my diving knife and I decided to draw a little blood to direct one of the bad boys closer to me. Let's just say, it worked, but almost too well. Had to let go of the tuna before it even got near because, had I held on any longer, I would've lost my hand along with the fish." He winced at the memory. "The shark came so hard, it knocked us both to the other side of the cage."

"Oh no. I have a feeling I know where this story is headed," Sicilia said.

"Yes," Roy said. "The idiot, STILL, is fixated on the eyes watching him through the glass. And he just got one-upped by his subordinate. So, he does the same thing, even though I try to warn him not to. The sharks are just getting too stirred up at this point. Well…he drew blood, extended a five-pound tuna out…I tried to physically pull him back, only to be pushed away. Shark moved in fast—" He clapped his hands together.

Sicilia covered her mouth. "Oh my—"

"It let go pretty quick. Griss got to keep his arm. Barely. Compound fracture along with multiple lacerations through skin, muscle, and tendons. Just a little pull, and that'd be all she wrote. So, let's just say that expedition ended a little prematurely for him."

"Amazing. Quite the interesting life you've had," she said. "I've got to travel around too, though not as extensively. And the work was not quite as exciting."

"You haven't mentioned what you do," Roy said.

"Did, rather. I'm done with it now. I was… in marketing. The object of desire selling outdoor equipment. Specifically, boats. I was good at getting results, apparently. Did photoshoots, commercials…"

Roy leaned forward. "Wait a sec…" He closed his eyes to remember the ad he once saw. He took a pose, as though showcasing a luxury yacht. "Thirty knot capability, carbon fiber construction, synthetic decking. So pretty on the outside, makes you wanna come inside…" He mimicked the come-hither look.

Sicilia nearly spat her wine. "Oh…my…"

"You know, if we weren't almost getting killed by fishermen today, I probably would've recognized you sooner."

"God. I was hoping that with your history of never being home, you'd have the luxury of *missing* those commercials," she said. She could feel the blood rushing to her face.

"Oh, come on. It's nothing to be embarrassed over," he said.

"Those stupid commercials," she muttered. "We got away with a lot. Of course, anyone who recognized me thought I was a slut who'd sleep with them." *Including my ex.*

"Bet it paid well, though."

"That it did."

"So, why'd you stop? Or are you just on a break?"

"No, I'm done. Just needed a change of pace," she said. "And a change in direction."

"Yeah? Any thoughts on what you wanna do? This island is a beautiful place, but I can't imagine you're planning on spending the rest of your days sitting on the beach watching the world go by... then again, now that I've heard myself say it out loud, maybe *you're* the smart one."

"Haven't really thought of it, lately," she said. "Who knows. Maybe I should study oceanography. Work on some research vessel."

"Very funny," he said.

"What makes you think I'm joking?" she said. "I'm sure there's a biologist out there who could use an assistant." She flashed her eyebrows at him. Roy's heart rate intensified.

He sipped on his wine. That sip quickly turned into him draining half the glass. He liked where things were going. Unfortunately, he'd been wrong once or twice in these little scenarios before. He could see that all arrows were pointing in the right direction, but was still afraid to give the desire reply, on the chance that his feelings were based on a misunderstanding, unlikely as that may be.

"I, uh...well, are you looking for long cruises? Or to work in a lab? Truth be told, it's a little of both. Maybe more than a little when it comes to the lab."

Sicilia chuckled. Even with the wine in his system, Roy was treading carefully. Most guys would've been trying to undress her before dinner. She liked manly men, and wasn't looking for a cuck, but unfortunately, too many moved on too quick, some even knowing she was married. These experiences made it hard to tell apart the guys who appreciated her as a person between those who saw her as a soulless object to have their way with.

"Sounds meaningful, though," Sicilia said. "Would you say it is?"

"Absolutely."

"Maybe that's one thing I've been lacking all this time."

"What else have you been lacking?"

She moved across the couch and answered his question. Lips touched, tongues swirled, and belt buckles were coming undone. The clothes left a trail as they made their way to the bedroom upstairs.

Already, this felt more natural and passionate than any of the so-called lovemaking with Bill. Yeah, she had just met Roy today. Nor did she care.

CHAPTER 13

Lucas turned the television volume up to hear it over the howl of the wind and crashing waves. All he could see outside was black, aside from the porch light which he usually kept off. Not like there were any burglars to warn away, aside from maybe the Glasses, and those idiots were cowards at the end of the day. Hence, they fled the moment a bullet came in their direction. Also, there was no chance they'd travel in this weather, considering the damage recently done to their vessel.

Lucas thought of the chase. It wasn't his first encounter with them. Unlike the biologists, he *had* witnessed the Glasses at their worst. They would happily cross anyone they believed had done them wrong. Luckily, they weren't able to get their hands on firearms. No reasonable seller would give it to them, and they didn't have the savvy to find an underground dealer. Underground fish markets, no problem. Hell, now that he thought of it, *they* were probably what killed that whale. Maybe it got caught up in a net, broke free, but got twisted around in the process. A bit of a stretch, but it was the most believable explanation he could come up with. And it matched the cruel behavior by the Glasses.

Starting tomorrow, though, he would have to keep an eye out for them. With a little luck, the Coast Guard would locate them and put an end to this, because if not, they'd likely be back for vengeance. Maybe not for him, but for the scientists and Sicilia. Lucas hated the idea of gunning a person down. He didn't even like action movies, except for maybe a few old Westerns. Still, when push came to shove and without help from authority figures, Lucas wouldn't hesitate to put someone down who was bent on potentially killing an innocent, let alone his treasured niece.

He put it all from his mind and turned up the volume a few more clicks. The room was dark, save for the light radiating from the television. On the screen was a Jimmy Stewart classic from 1950 called *Broken Arrow,* a story of an ex-soldier attempting to make peace between Arizona settlers and Cochise's Apaches after ten years of war. Two factions making peace—*Ha! Couldn't be more relevant today, considering the culture war.* He had half a mind to try and somehow get this movie to everyone in the country. Then again, half would probably whine and cry about the technical details, or the fact that Jeff Chandler was not actually Native American, rather than see the bigger picture. That led his thoughts to other things, which ultimately made him all the more happy to be separated from it all. He'd heard many people, especially in the last year, state how they'd just love to move to a private island and get away from everything going on. And here Lucas Instone was, living that very dream.

Even if there was a storm outside. Could be worse, though. At least it wasn't at hurricane proportions. At least the storm damage would be minimal. That would be the icing on the cake after the day he'd had. Several gallons of fuel used, and not a dollar made to make up for it.

Still, Sicilia was home. That was a win. On top of that, he was confident that better days were ahead. With that in mind, he crossed his bare feet on the ottoman and leaned back in the chair. After thirty seconds, his troubles evaporated and he was lost in the movie.

Meanwhile, the wind continued its assault. Thunder cracked so loudly overhead that it rumbled the house. Nothing Lucas wasn't used to. He sipped his wine and kept his eyes on the movie. He wasn't much of an alcohol drinker, but today he made an exception. Glancing at the time, he was certain Sicilia and Roy were in the middle of their date by now.

It's just dinner. It's just dinner. It's just—Oh, who am I kidding? He downed the glass. *She's an adult. Can't change that. And adults tend to get together and...* "Let's not finish that thought," he said aloud. "However, I *will* refill this glass." It was doing the job, and it was hitting the spot.

There was another crack of thunder. Lightning glimpsed through the window, briefly lighting the dark room. Lucas ignored it, fixated on the scenery on screen. The dialogue exchanged between Stewart's character and Cochise was very hypnotic to him on this viewing. Then again, he was also filling himself with wine.

There was another crack of thunder, which again failed to divert his attention. Behind that reverberating *crack* was a heavy *crash!* That got his attention.

Lucas jumped to his feet, inadvertently spilling his glass onto the carpet. That was the least of his concerns at the moment. That second sound was *not* thunder. Whatever it was, it came from the direction of the shore, and sounded more like a heavy impact of some kind, like a car wreck.

He considered all possibilities. There were no trees by the dock, so one couldn't have fallen on it or his boat. Even if one was close, it'd have to be one heck of a heavy tree for an impact that heavy. The *Europa* was on the other side of the peninsula, as were Sicilia's vessels. His boat was well secured, leaving no possibility that the wind might have rocked it against the dock.

In Lucas' eyes, there was only one possibility. He might have been wrong about the Glasses. Not only were they coming back for revenge, but they were directing their efforts toward *him.* No sense in wasting time calling the Coast Guard. By the time he made that call, they'd likely be long gone. He grabbed his .30-06, loaded it, and moved to the front door. As he did, he heard another crunching sound. This one wasn't as loud, and didn't seem like a crash, but the groaning of a structure coming apart.

He flashed the outside light, then peered out the corner of the window. There was brief movement at the dock, though he couldn't see what. Even with the light, it was too dark. He couldn't even make out the shape of the silhouette. All he knew was that whatever it was, it was big. At least as big as a boat. With nothing else out there, that *had* to be what it was.

Lucas launched himself into the storm and rushed his yard, his rifle aimed as though ready to combat an invasion of enemy soldiers. There was nothing but darkness in front of him. There was no sound other than those created by the storm. There was no motor, no engine, no further crashing. But something was off. There was a strange smell permeating the air. Whatever it was, it was vile. He could only describe it as a combination of burning rubber combined with rotting flesh.

With rain breaking over his body, he continued to approach the dock. Only when the lightning flashed again did he stop.

The dock was completely decimated. Only the section nearest to the shore stood intact, the rest, however, was in ruins and washing up on his beach. His boat was still there, secured only by the port quarter mooring line which was secured to the section of dock still standing. Forty feet of hard wood, which had survived category five hurricanes, was completely crunched.

His heart thumped and his hands shook, along with the muzzle of the rifle they held. This wasn't caused by the Glasses. They didn't have the means. And certainly, they wouldn't be able to escape without at least being heard. Not even in this storm.

Lucas cautiously approached the shoreline, then knelt down to inspect one of the fragments. Several boards were broken down the middle, others splintered in various pieces. Looking to his right, he saw a log-shaped object in the sand. When the lightning flashed again, he realized it was the foot of the exterior pillars. It was about three feet long, and covered in grime. It had been ripped from place, as though by a crane. The Glasses didn't have a crane on their boat, and no winch would've yanked that out from the earth without him hearing it. And how on earth did they break the post in two? The wood was almost a foot thick and extremely durable. It had to be; it was designed not only to maintain the structure of the dock, but to hold a large vessel in place.

Even more odd; it reeked of that strange odor.

The sound of splashing water in the distance made him back away. Lucas shone a flashlight into the ocean. The waves had doubled in size…all of which were directly in front of him. He took a moment to pan side-to-side. The waves further north and south were shallower. Yet, the ones lapping at his feet were huge. It was as though something enormous was pushing them forward. He continued aiming his light outward, but he saw nothing but an angry storm and floating wreckage.

Lucas tried to convince himself that the wine had gone straight to his head. It didn't work. He could feel the presence of something out there. He felt something else too; something he hadn't felt in many years. Fear.

As though permeating from that fear, that horrible smell returned. The wind was pushing it into his face, making sure he didn't miss its existence. It was worse than before. It was like a geyser filled with some putrid fumes of rotting corpses was erupting from a mass grave.

"Lord of all creation," he muttered. He still couldn't see anything, but at this point he no longer cared to identify the source. He spun on his heel and rushed to the safety of his home. He shut the movie off, switched on a lamp in the corner, then watched the shore as best as he could. The outside light was still on, though its glow could barely reach the shoreline.

A hundred thoughts raged, creating another storm, this time inside his head. What could he do? What *should* he do? Lucas usually had all the answers, but nothing about this scenario made sense. He thought of making a radio call to the authorities, but what would he say? 'Help, my dock is destroyed, and there's a strange smell'? They'd just brush it off as storm damage and residue from the ocean life.

He thought about his niece. Should he warn her? Again, warn her of what? He didn't even know what he was hiding from—if he was hiding from anything at all. Still, he wanted her to be on guard.

He searched for his phone. It was hard to see in the dark, and there was no landline on the island. Back in the day, he and his brother would use two-way radios to communicate, but they quit working sometime in the last two years, and Lucas never truly bothered to replace them. To make matters worse, when he did finally locate his cell phone, it failed to call out. Service out this far was spotty at best. And in *this* weather? There was no way of reaching Sicilia.

There was only one other option: trek over there on foot and let her and Roy know something was going on.

He passed through the kitchen into a hallway that led to the back entrance. The door flung from his grip the instant it came unlatched. Lucas didn't bother trying to shut it, instead running straight for the hill. He only made a few steps before another sound of impact halted him.

It was the same kind of sound that initially alerted his attention. He turned to his right and looked again to the shore, his eye trained along his iron sights. The next flash of lightning revealed his fishing vessel floating away freely. Not only was it floating away, but the bow was dipping into the ocean. Even with a brief glimpse, he understood what was happening. The boat was taking on water!

"What the—"

A zig-zag of light creased across the world of black clouds. With its brief illumination, Lucas identified two other things: the rest of the dock had collapsed, and there was something protruding from the water in its place. There was no word to describe it other than 'huge'. There was a sticky sound, mixed with that of debris fragments thudding against each other. With only the porchlight providing any visual, he couldn't see much from where he stood. Only a vague shape. Only with the crunching of wood and sand did he realize that, whatever it was, it was coming up the beach.

It was alive.

Lucas had a split-second to make a choice. Barricade himself in the house, or make a run for Sicilia's house. He chose the closer option. He dashed through the open doorway, then fought against the wind to shut the door behind him. He latched and locked it, then hurried back into the living room. He shut the lamp off, coating himself in total darkness.

There was the sound of shattering glass. The outside light went dark. With his rifle gripped tightly, he peered out through the corner of the window. He couldn't see it. Right when he needed it most, the cursed lightning wouldn't flash.

The horrid smell had now entered the house. There was a wet, sticky sound outside, along with a grinding motion. Whatever was out there, it didn't walk on legs. It seemed to glide, almost like a snake.

Then there was silence. Lucas remained silent. The smell was still there, meaning *it* was still there. His finger quivered over the trigger. He whispered a prayer. The lightning finally flashed.

He peered out the window. Nothing was in the front yard. He exhaled slowly, then considered the possibility that it had returned to the sea. With that in mind, he started for the hallway. He entered the kitchen, located on the south side of the house, then found the juncture to the hallway. Before making the turn, he froze, his eyes locked on the odd violet glow radiating in the window. It was dim and circular, almost like a ring, with little veiny lines in the black center. Like a pupil.

Only when that ring shifted did Lucas realize he was staring at an eye. Darkness didn't protect him, as the beast watching him was born in darkness. The window imploded, smothering the kitchen with glass. Huge sticky appendages ripped at the frame, shredding the wall with the ease of peeling a banana. Even in the dark, Lucas could make out the shape of the worm-like arms extending toward him. He could hear a suctioning sound, that seemed harmonious with the sounds of slithering wetness.

Yelling for God's grace and forgiveness for all his life's sins, Lucas took aim and opened fire.

****

Sicilia shot up out of bed. A split-second ago, she had nearly drifted off, lost in a world of bliss in the arms of her new lover. Now she was alert, staring out the window toward the east.

"Did you hear that?" she asked. Roy, who was equally drowsy after their vigorous activity, leaned up.

"I think it was thunder," he said. "Don't tell me you're afraid of storms." There was another loud crack in the distance. This time, his brain registered it. It was more of a *pop* than anything else. A gunshot, coming from Uncle Lucas' property.

"Oh, Jesus!" Sicilia threw herself out of bed, threw on her jeans and a sweatshirt then hurried downstairs. She didn't bother putting on shoes.

"Damn it," Roy said. He got his naked self out of bed and searched for the light so he could find his clothes.

****

Lucas kicked his heels against the floor, keeping his rifle pointed down toward the window. The thing had moved off, leaving a gaping hole in the wall. He continued scooting backwards until he was in the living room. The wind and rain were quickly invading the breach, making it difficult to hear anything. But behind the sounds of angry weather was movement, except he couldn't pinpoint it. He got to his feet and peered out the main window. All he could see was black.

Then the lightning flashed. The towering, rounded bulk, was right outside the glass, its face without emotion, even in its single eye. With the return of darkness, the tentacles lashed, reducing the window to shards.

A wet, rubbery tightness gripped his body. Like a python, the appendage constricted. Lucas shook in its grasp, his bones crunching, the splinters piercing internal organs, the air being forced from his lungs. Then there was the sensation of wind and rain as he was pulled out into the open. Every muscle tightened, including his trigger finger, sending a round into the sky before the weapon fell from his grasp.

Finally, he let out a cry of pain.

His final sensation was that of ocean water and being submerged.

****

Sicilia ascended the small elevation between the properties. Rain assaulted her eyes and the wind invaded her ears. Still, despite the storm's attempts to shield her, she recognized the sound of gunfire and destruction.

She reached the peak of the elevation and screamed. "Uncle Lucas!" She could see the house and the enormous gap in the south side. Debris covered the side yard. It had been ripped *out*. Already, the wind went to work scattering the fragments.

Screaming his name again, she started down the small hill, only to slip and tumble. She fell head over heels, only to crash against the base of a tree. The world spun. Her temples throbbed. Rolling to her hands and knees, she crawled toward the house, only to lock her eyes on the ocean.

The flash of lightning betrayed its presence. Several meters out, she saw its leathery, rounded body. Other shapes, snake-like, danced around it, cutting through the water like serpents. Then, as fast as the lightning, it had disappeared.

She tried to get up, but fell down.

"Lucas!"

She heard footsteps behind her, then felt a pair of hands scoop under her armpits and lift her up.

"Jesus, Sicilia, you okay?! You hit your head pretty good," Roy said, looking her over. She pushed him away and staggered toward the house. Roy used his iPhone light to get a clearer view of the damage. "Oh my God. Mr. Instone?!"

Sicilia hurried into the house. "Uncle Lucas?! OW!" She dropped to the floor, rolled onto her rear, and checked her foot. A two-inch jagged piece of glass protruded out.

Roy, who had his shoes on, rushed to her side again. He lifted her up and carried her over the glass.

"It took him!" she cried. "That thing! It took him!"

"What? What thing?" he said.

"I don't know what it is, but it was huge! A *monster*!"

Roy looked at the cut on her forehead. She had hit herself good and was clearly hazy.

"Stay here."

He ran back inside, calling for Lucas as he checked all of the rooms. He then exited through the front door. He checked the yard, the shed, and the dock—the latter of which was no longer there, along with the boat, which was sinking several hundred feet out.

But no Lucas.

Roy stood, the rain pelting his face, unable to see and hear anything, except the howl of the storm and the cries of Sicilia Instone.

CHAPTER 14

It was nine in the evening when Roy ordered Brett to make an emergency call to the U.S. Coast Guard. Unfortunately, it wasn't until dawn when they were able to arrive, as the cutter in the area was busy with two yachts that were taking on water during the storm. At around eight in the morning, the hundred-and-ten foot Island-Class Cutter *Horizon Flare* arrived at Diamond Green.

The investigation, led by Commander Thomas Rhea, went underway immediately. Testimonies were taken, the house thoroughly looked through, and the shallow region dredged. Divers were deployed to raise Lucas' vessel.

Rhea had seen and heard many strange things during his time in the Coast Guard. He intercepted drug smugglers coming in from Colombia, performed several rescue and recovery dives, seen vessels sunk by collision, explosion, and mechanical failures. He'd seen bodies torn to shreds by sharks and crustaceans, though in most cases it had occurred over a period of time. He heard the testimonies of drunken seafarers, some even stating they saw aliens on the horizon. This was the first time he was given the story of a sea monster that arose from the depths to snatch a human victim and haul him off into the sea.

There was no denying the odd damage done to the building, not to mention the dock. But the storm had wiped away much of the evidence of what had occurred. All that remained was the sunken boat, the remaining fragments of the dock, the house, and the body of a baby sperm whale beached along the eastern side of the peninsula.

Even the marine biologist, Roy Brinkman, seemed puzzled to the dead animal's presence.

Roy stood on the beach, sleep deprived, frustrated, impatient, and worst of all, confused. Twelve hours ago, he was sure he'd wake up this morning feeling like a new man. He certainly didn't expect the turn the night ultimately took. Gunshots, wreckage, Lucas Instone gone, this dead whale mysteriously appearing, and the odd smell that lingered on for several hours. It was gone now, which was unfortunate; it at least would've been noted by the Commander as an oddity.

Roy looked over his shoulder at Sicilia, who was seated on a folding chair near the propane tank. Her face was red and her hair was a mess, and she still wore the same clothes she hastily threw on last night, the only addition being a bra so not to attract the lingering eyes of the seamen. Her eyes displayed fury and despair, aimed at the sea and these assholes who clearly didn't believe her story.

Roy worried that those feelings were also directed at him. Though he never outright said he didn't believe her, he didn't back her up either. A fact made abundantly clear by Commander Rhea's next question.

"She told us she witnessed a large animal in the water." The Commander struggled to keep a straight face. "You were with her. Did you see any... let's just call it 'strange movement' in the water? Any presence of any kind?"

Roy shook his head. "I arrived after."

"And *that* wasn't here when you arrived?" Rhea pointed to the whale.

"No, sir. As of yesterday afternoon, when I was standing right there on that deck, there was no whale," Roy said. *I already answered this question.* Then again, he couldn't deny that this situation was weird for the officer as well. Worse yet, the divers found no evidence of Lucas Instone's body. For over five hours, they had been searching vigorously, only to find no trace.

The Commander waited for the divers on the south side to make their radio call.

"Unit Two, reporting a negative find."

"Copy. Return to home plate." Rhea lowered the radio. "Damn it."

"So, what now?" Roy asked.

Rhea shook his head. "This is what we know: The boat was found over five hundred yards out. Assuming Mr. Instone was on it when it went down, he could've been swept anywhere southwest of here by the current. The waters only get deeper for several miles, and it's a big area to search."

Sicilia stood up and march over. "He *wasn't* on the boat!"

"Ma'am, did you see him at all last night when you arrived?"

"I heard him. I heard gunshots!"

"Which could've been fired from the vessel," Rhea said.

"Kind of a long shot, Commander."

"Didn't you state he used the weapon in self-defense when fending off your attackers yesterday?"

"I—yes. But how do you explain *this*?" Roy pointed at the house.

"You said yourself he made enemies. It makes perfect sense they retaliated. Perhaps they used the storm as cover."

"Oh, give me a break. They'd need a freaking tank to do something like this," Roy said. "Look here. This was pulled *out.*"

"I'm not denying it looks strange, but it's the only lead we have, sir," the Commander replied. His demeanor was calm, but the slow manner in which he spoke indicated he was fed up with this investigation. Not that he wasn't sympathetic, but he knew there were no answers that would satisfy these civilians. "Listen. The storm wiped away a lot of the evidence. We have a battered dead whale showing up the same day the victim's boat and dock was wrecked. We have precedence to consider this was done by human hands, even if a few details don't add up."

"It wasn't them," Sicilia said.

"Ma'am. You admitted it was dark and that you hit your head running over here. Then add the shock of seeing this place in ruins. With the storm in your face, it's likely your mind played tricks on you."

Sicilia moved toward him, her fist balled up. Roy grabbed her wrist.

Don't. PLEASE don't.

She eased up.

"Ma'am, I'm not trying to be insulting. But you've got to look at this from my perspective," the Commander said.

"What about the body?" Roy asked.

"At this point, it's like finding a needle in a haystack," the Commander said. "I've got a response unit on the way. They'll remain on site until the investigation is complete. I have orders to patrol the nearby waters and see if I can find the perpetrators. With no other leads, there's no other action I can take."

"Anything you need from us?" Roy asked. "Am I free to continue my work?"

"If you wish to do so, I'm not gonna stop you. If you have any problems, or by some miracle find additional clues, contact my unit on Twelve." Commander Rhea offered his hand. "I'm sorry I can't do more."

Roy shook it. Sicilia didn't bother. She turned and marched inland. Roy shook his head. *NOT what I was hoping today would be like.* He chased after her.

"Hey, Sicilia. You alright?"

She scoffed. "You heard that prick."

"Listen, they went all through the house. Your uncle's not in there. They didn't find him in the boat, and they've been all around the island. Considering the current…"

"He didn't get washed away. He was *taken*! I saw it," she said.

"What was it, exactly?" he said. "What the hell was it you think you saw?" She spun on her heel and met him with a furious stare. Roy slapped his pant leg, looked up at the sky, silently begging for God's help in this situation, then corrected his wording. "What was it you saw?"

"It had arms. Several of them, like tentacles. It had a large body, like a big potato bag—" She noticed Roy's inquisitive gaze. "It looked like a giant fucking octopus, okay?!"

Roy closed his eyes. *Not quite the help I was looking for, God.* After everything they had gone through, now he had to add her theory of a giant cephalopod to the mix. What the hell could he say to that?! He didn't want to disagree and risk pissing her off even further. Yet, he didn't want to blindly agree. After all, she did in fact hit her head, and the storm would've caused a lot of disorientation. Also, he couldn't deny the Commander's assessment of her head injury. It wasn't severe, but it would've added to the confusion at the time. Roy was in a lose-lose situation.

He didn't have to express his disbelief, since his delay confirmed those feelings to Sicilia. She groaned, then kicked up sand as she marched home.

Roy ran after her. "Si, wait!"

"Fuck yourself."

"Oh, come on! Listen, I'm here to help."

"Give me a break," she said. "Just take your drone and go."

"I—" Roy stopped at the peak of the hill, unsure of what to say. The only thing more awkward than being interrogated by the Coast Guard was talking to the express delivery person who brought the drone. When the guy arrived on his boat, he certainly wasn't expecting to see a Coast Guard cutter in the area. Roy, despite all the other things on his mind, was surprised the overnight delivery got here so fast.

Money talks, I guess. Maybe if we paid the government fifty-grand, they'd send someone as fast.

The box containing the drone was on the dock. Brett had taken the time to examine the components. Might as well, since there wasn't anything he could offer to the investigation. He had his headphones on all night. Personally, he thought Sicilia was going crazy; an opinion Roy warned him to keep to himself.

Roy decided to go after Sicilia again. She was in her shed now, sorting through some items.

"What can I do to help?" he asked. When he arrived at the shed, he noticed she was getting her speargun and accessories out. There were two scuba tanks, flippers, as well as a large chain. Lying beside the chain was the tri-hook, courtesy of the Glasses. "Mind telling me what you're planning?"

"What do you care?"

"Si, listen. You know I'm on your side."

"Didn't seem like it a few minutes ago."

"What do you expect? For me to lie? I *didn't* see anything!"

Sicilia kicked the door. Despite the knee-jerk reaction, she still took a moment to consider his position. It was difficult, as all she could think of was her uncle's distinct screams, and the sight of that horrible creature wading into the sea. It wasn't a trick of the imagination. She saw it. She knew she saw it. Not once, but twice.

"I understand," she simply said. She picked up her items and began carrying them to her father's fishing vessel.

"I'd still like to know what the hell it is you're planning to do?"

"I'm gonna hunt the bastard down," she said.

"Listen…"

"Stop fucking telling me to *listen*!" she snapped. Roy raised his hands in surrender. Again, he had to look at it from her perspective. She came home for the first time in years, reunited with her uncle—her *last* family member, only to have him taken away that same day. On top of that, she had to endure people calling her crazy. It wasn't said in so many words, but the sentiment was obvious.

With nothing else to do, Roy picked up the hook and chain and carried it to her vessel. Might as well. Not like he'd be able to stop her. He just hoped the small gesture would somehow put her at ease. Instead, it invited a question he REALLY didn't want asked.

"You going to help?"

"Help? With—"

"Give me a break. Like you don't know! Help me *hunt* the damn thing!"

"I don't even know where to begin," Roy said. "We don't even know what it is you're looking for. If it's even—if…"

"Yeah, I get it. You don't believe it's there. That's fine. I'll go myself," she said. "I know I saw it. *Twice.*"

"Can we please just talk about—twice?"

"Yeah. Yesterday, right before we met, I saw something huge move under the water. That's why I was on edge and speared your drone. That time, I thought my eyes were playing tricks on me. But after last night…" Sicilia took her dive suit into the house to change. "I know what I saw."

"Si, take it from a marine biologist. No species of cephalopod that large exist."

"Yeah? What was it that killed that whale?"

Roy stammered. "I'm gonna look into that. *Probably* the Glasses. I wouldn't be surprised if those were propellor wounds." *Though, I can't really explain why the thing's so twisted up.*

He followed her up the stairs, only to be stopped midway up.

"You need something?"

"No. I'm just checking on you. I don't think you should be alone right now."

"I'm getting changed. Don't need your help with that."

"No, that's not what I meant."

Sicilia made a shooing motion. "Go off in your boat. Play with your new toy." She raced up to her bedroom and slammed the door.

Realizing he was no longer desired in this household, Roy exited the house and returned to his boat. Brett was now on deck, still looking over the various accessories to the new drone. He looked up as Roy climbed aboard.

"Trouble in paradise?"

Roy looked at him with disgust. "Really, man?"

"That bad, huh?"

"Dude, think for a sec," Roy said. "Her uncle was just killed. On top of that, we have no freaking clue how! She thinks she saw something. Personally, I don't know what to think."

"Her eyes were probably just playing tricks on her."

"Don't say that too loud," Roy said. "Regardless, I think we better leave her alone. Nothing much we can do regarding the case. Coast Guard can't find anything. Not like they haven't tried."

"They sticking around?"

Roy nodded. "They'll be in the area. There's a response boat coming in from North Key. They'll essentially be standing guard while *Horizon Flare* conducts a search of the southern waters. Nothing they can really do at this point, except go out looking for the Glasses." He went for the bridge. "Check the lines. We still have a job to do. Probably the only way I'll be able to get my mind off the craziness."

"Where we going?" Brett asked.

"Two miles east, the depth gets to four thousand feet. I'd like to start searching there, now that we have improved equipment."

"Don't worry about it, man," Brett said. He held up the drone. "If she bought you this, she *really* digs you. Unfortunately, life threw a curveball into your romance. Just give her time to mourn her tragedy. Things might still work out."

Roy wasn't sure how to respond. It was a day-long romance at most. So far, it was looking like it wasn't something that would go beyond a one-night-stand. He certainly wanted it to go further, but Brett was right about the curveball. Maybe it was too good to be true.

The only way to force it from his mind was to work. He started the engine and throttled the boat to the east.

****

Sicilia stood at the window, watching the *Europa* move away from her dock. In the moment, she felt pushing him away would somehow help with her feelings. There were few things she could control, little power she held. Instead, she added regret to the long lists of emotions she was feeling right now.

She couldn't sit around. She had to do something. She stripped her clothes off and got into her wetsuit, then tied her hair back. There was one thing left to do before boarding her dad's vessel. *My boat*, she reminded herself.

She returned to Uncle Lucas' house. The Coast Guard had departed, the cutter already disappearing to the south. Didn't matter. She didn't need them anyway.

She was careful to avoid the bits of broken glass still on the floor. Her foot was still sore from the glass cut, though nothing she couldn't handle. The pain that truly affected her was the realization that this was the first actual time she'd set foot in Lucas' house in ten years. She never got to have her dinner with him. She hoped for a wave of nostalgia when stepping in, not grief. Still, she put the childhood memories to use.

There was a stairway on the north side, which led up to the bedrooms. She ascended and slowly entered Lucas' room. She didn't bother gazing at any of the belongings that would never be touched by him again. All she was interested in was the cabinet near the west window. She opened it.

There they were, his *Smith & Wesson* .38 revolver and *Browning* pump action shotgun. Uncle Lucas was by no means violent, but at the same time, he was a believer in self-defense.

Sorry, Uncle. I know you wouldn't approve if you were here, but I'm not letting that thing get away with this. She took the revolver. It felt heavy in her grip; a reminder that she hadn't handled firearms in a long while. Still, she remembered how to remove the cylinder. She loaded it, stuffed it in its holster, then checked the shotgun. Once again, she had to play around with it until she remembered how to load the shells into the port. Slowly, it was coming back to her.

She pumped the shotgun, then took it and the revolver to her fishing boat. For the next hour or so, she loaded her vessel with her uncle's fishing supplies. Then came the last step. Bait.

With a large knife, she walked toward the whale carcass. She gazed at its huge head. Circular marks, similar to those left behind from suction cups—like those from a squid or octopus.

"So, you like the taste of whale, huh?" she muttered. She took her knife and drove it into the flesh. Sneering, she sawed away, wetting her dive suit in blood until a three-foot chunk of the whale's flesh came free. She was surprised at the sheer weight of the meat as she picked it up. These creatures truly were heavy, even in their youth. Good—all the more likely it would catch the attention of the monster.

Now, it was time to hunt.

CHAPTER 15

"Yes, sir. Destination is in sight… Affirmative. Orders confirmed: resume patrol around the island until further orders. Copy. Out."

Ensign Ralf Willis placed the radio down and spun the helm, taking the boat around the north side of the island. He could hear a drizzling sound behind him. Glancing over his shoulder, he could see his fellow guardsman urinating over the transom of the forty-one foot U.S.C.G. response boat.

"Seriously, man? You wait until we're on site to do that?"

Ensign Jacob Anthony zipped up and moaned with relief. "Sorry. That energy drink decided it wanted to escape all of a sudden."

"Shouldn't be bringing that stuff aboard. The Commander'll kill ya."

"He'll never know," Jacob said.

Ralf stared at him. "Wait…you didn't…"

"Won't confirm or deny the current presence of the can."

"Great. Litter the ocean," Ralf said. Jacob scoffed. The guardsman, who was six years his junior, was always uptight about these kinds of things. Jacob always assumed it was because of the chick he was trying to impress back in Key Elliot.

"Oh, quit being such an idealist," Jacob said. "She's not here to swoon over your 'save-the-earth' routine."

"It's not just being an idealist. This island is private property," Ralf said. "If the owner sees you do anything stupid, we'll be dead meat."

"Good. Maybe we'd be grounded," Jacob replied. He leaned over the transom. He was bored out of his mind. The trip from the mainland felt longer than ever. The issues went deeper than that—he simply didn't even want to be here. He resented his father for forcing him into the Coast Guard. Then again, it was either this or the marines, or be out on the street. Of course, he had the misconception that the training in the U.S.C.G. was a cakewalk compared to the rest of the military. Surprisingly, it wasn't. Unfortunately, no amount of discipline would purge his bitterness. He was just a man in his mid-twenties biding his time. At least, he was a man in the sense that he was full-grown.

Ralf, who was twenty-years old, couldn't stand working with this idiot. He couldn't believe he was younger, yet more mature than this asshole. Why did the Coast Guard accept this idiot? His uniform looked like crap; he barely shaved, he was late to formation and drills. Twice, he had been reprimanded. His poor attitude was just the icing on top of the shit cake. Yet, he always behaved just well enough to keep himself from being kicked out. It was clear that Jacob knew, despite his feelings and behavior, that an early discharge wouldn't look good on his resume, and that afterwards he'd have to find a job, because no way in hell was his dad letting him live in the house any longer. Thus, he was stuck, with no way to be happy. He wanted to coast by, but coasting by also meant boredom. Then again, he had no desire to be on the choppers, rescuing people in storms, or dealing with smugglers. He hated it all. Same with college and retail. Perhaps, it was just the self-defeating feeling of a man with no sense of purpose.

Ralf pitied him in a way. He loved being in the Coast Guard. He didn't mind little jobs like this. In eighteen months, he'd be reporting to the Coast Guard Training Center in Pensacola, Florida to become a helicopter pilot. Just had another three semesters of school to finish up in the meantime. Until then, he'd have to deal with people like Jacob Anthony.

"So, what'd the Commander say?" Jacob asked.

"Just to stay in the area and report any unusual activity or findings," Ralf said.

"The hell would constitute an unusual finding? A mermaid?"

"Anything pertaining to the case, I guess," Ralf said.

"So, in other words, hang out until told otherwise." Jacob spat into the water.

"That's the job," Ralf said.

Jacob snorted. "Just need to get through the next thirty-months. Gosh, it feels longer when it's put like that." They circled around the east side of the island. There, they saw a sixty-foot fishing vessel moving north. Ralf offered a wave, but it went unnoticed.

His companion chuckled. "Looks like she doesn't want us here either."

"Someone was killed during the storm. I think she's the family member living on the island," Ralf said. "She's probably not in a good mood."

"Most natives aren't," Jacob replied. "I can think of a way to cheer her up, though." He clicked his tongue.

"Yeah, good luck with that," Ralf said.

"Better luck than you'll have trying to impress that vegan chick," Jacob said. "I've been trying to warn you about those. Don't trust the soy."

Ralf sighed. "Can't deny that. Shit tastes like cardboard." He turned to the right, then slowed the boat. "Holy shit. No wonder she's in a bad mood. Look at that."

Jacob moved to the starboard railing. "Something went down, that's for sure. Did the Commander say exactly what happened?"

"'Cause unknown' is all I was given."

Jacob took a seat and crossed his legs. "Well, I hope they figure it out soon. Because in about four hours we'll have to turn back."

"There'll be a tugboat here by then," Ralf said. He glanced back at the pathetic guardsman. "You might as well pretend to like the job. It doesn't get better from here. Can't hope to coast your way through life. Sooner or later, action is bound to come your way, and when it does, it'll be out of left field. You won't be ready for it, because you're so used to doing nothing."

Jacob chuckled. *Kid thinks he's in Iraq.* "Speak for yourself, kid. You might be all hot-under-the-collar to get a piece of the action. Joke's on you, Willis. Kids like you are the first to get killed."

Ralf didn't reply. No sense in debating with someone like Jacob Anthony. The guy will milk his veteran status for all its worth, getting free meals, and *maybe* some female attention. Unfortunately, some might actually be dumb enough to believe any bullshit story he would tell. Same for potential employers.

As long as he's out of my hair. Ralf continued patrolling around the island. One thing he couldn't help but agree with Jacob on—it was a boring assignment.

CHAPTER 16

"Alright. Buoy Nineteen is set and activated. Temperature reading at sixty-seven. Now that that's set, I'm ready to deploy the drone. Ready when you are, Doc."

Brett took the controls again to test the mechanical arms of the device. They reached out like crabs' claws. With a shift in the joystick, the device moved forward. From up above, the yellow thing looked like a three-foot long crustacean with jet propulsion at the rear and a camera lens where its eyes ought to be.

Roy had taken them a little too far; closer to three miles rather than two. And just like when he was at the helm, he seemed to be lost in a trance. He took a seat near the transom and was staring far out into the infinite blue. The water lapped at the hull, far calmer than it had been hours earlier. Yet, inside, he was more tense. It was odd for Brett to see him like this. The doctor was the most dedicated marine biologist he had ever met. Yet, today, he seemed as though he wanted to be anywhere but here.

"Um. Surface level toxins are negative. I suppose that's a good sign," Brett said. Again, he failed to get Roy's attention. Another rarity occurred: Brett Rollins lost his patience. He slammed his fist on the gunwale, making Roy jump. "Hey!"

"Whoa!"

"Earth to Doctor Brinkman? Anyone there?"

"I was listening," Roy said.

"HA!" Brett held his stomach. "Doc, you're good at many things. Lying is not one of them."

"Appreciate your motivational speech," Roy said.

"I know you're thinking of pretty-diver-lady…" Brett said.

"Her name is Sicilia," Roy retorted.

"Yeah-yeah. To me, she'll always be Pretty-diver-lady. Scratch it: it's Pretty-diver-lady-with-a-speargun. Better yet, maybe it ought to be Pretty-diver-lady-with-a-speargun-who-shoots-drones-and-is-Dr.-Brinkman's-first-booty-call-since-college."

"You're a real jackass, you know that?" Roy said. He stood up. "AND, for your information, it's not my first time since college."

"Yeah? Second or third then?" Brett said.

"You—I—shut up!" Roy said. He finally broke a smile. "It's been a long, weird night, man. I can't get it out of my head."

Brett came close to making a comedic retort of "the sex or the storm?" but managed to hold back. A man did die after all. A good man at that.

Really need to check that brain-to-mouth filter.

"Well, then you can take the controls," he said instead. Roy sniggered.

"You complain whenever I do that. You're the control freak, after all."

"Oh yeah. Me. *I'm* the control freak," Brett said. He moved away from the lab desk, offering it to the boss. "Nah, you take the controls today. Actually doing this yourself will force you to take your mind off everything going on. Plus, you won't have to worry about me hogging all the credit when we find something." Roy made an exasperated sigh, pretending to be annoyed. As usual, Brett saw right through it. Roy stepped forward and took the seat. As he grasped the control console, he felt his assistant tap his shoulder and lean forward. "By the way, Doc, she *bought* you this crazy expensive drone. Believe me, she still digs you. Considering you made that big of an impression in a matter of hours—less than that, really—my advice is to give her some time. She'll come back around."

Roy nodded. *Damn it. Don't make me say something sentimental like 'thank you'.* He wanted to, though. Deep down, the guy actually had some heart—though its arteries were probably getting clogged by that microwaved crap he ate.

"Watch the winch," he said. "We've got four thousand feet of tether. Don't want to risk it getting tangled up."

"Standing by," Brett said.

Roy initiated descent. The winch slowly turned, unwinding the cable as the drone plunged into the depths. Roy watched as the golden sunlight faded into shades of green and blue. At two hundred feet, he had to rely on the depth readers. He didn't want to shine his lights too early, as that would drain the unit's power.

He got more antsy with each added foot. Part of him wondered what he would see. Would there be an abundance of life, or a dead zone full of discarded barrels. It was unlikely that he'd find something in this exact spot, as it would be like firing blind into an open field, yet managing to hit a bullseye. It would take time and a little bit of patience.

At three-thousand-six-hundred feet, he engaged the lights. What he saw was a world of rocks and sand, not quite as dramatic as the thermal vents one would see in the extreme depths, such as the Mariana Trench. Still, despite being bland, it was still amazing to witness. The crazy thing to think was that this was a relatively shallow area in the ocean—the average depth was twelve-thousand feet.

That realization made Roy question whether he was wasting his time or not. Why would the company dump *here*? Yeah, it was still deep, but in comparison to most areas, it was an odd choice. Maybe the paper mill was looking for a cheap place to dump, thus, they didn't want to go too far out.

The levels of dioxin are too high. The source HAS to be near here.

He steered the drone along the ocean depths. There were no fish that he could see. No rays, anglerfish, viper fish, or squid. The tether was almost stretched to the max, forcing Roy to keep the drone thirty feet or so above the water. He wouldn't be able to scrape up samples, but that was of no consequence. He needed to *see* if any barrels had been dumped here.

So far, he saw nothing but ocean floor.

"Brett, take the helm. Take us ahead, slowly. We're gonna be here a while."

****

Sicilia watched the red trail stretch out into the horizon. The mixture of fish guts swirled in the bucket by her right knee, rippling as red droplets fell from the scoop. There was a splash of thick liquid as she plunged it into the bucket, then added the scoopful of guts to the trail.

Her eyes hardly blinked. For the hour or so that she spent chumming, they were locked on the trail and the buoy that floated near it. The chain rattled, intent on sinking, only to be forcefully kept at the surface by the floatation device. The chum trail obscured the red piece of meat from view. Like a fish bobber, she waited for that buoy to vanish and the chain to go taut.

That hour turned into two.

Nothing.

She was maybe a mile northeast from Diamond Green, which now resembled a thin greenish-white line in the horizon. She glanced at her shotgun and speargun, both of which were leaning against the transom, ready to be snatched up.

"Where are you?" she muttered.

****

The drumming of the motor tempted Roy to doze off. He'd hardly slept the previous night, and as fantastic as the ocean floor was, there wasn't enough visual stimulation to keep his attention. Once or twice, he'd see a few Humboldt squids, and some illuminated fish, but not enough to keep his mind sharp. He needed something to help snap him into focus. At this point, he'd take anything. A walk, rock music, even a reasonable burst of pain, as long as it got the blood rushing. A decent conversation would probably help. Unfortunately, the only other person on board was his assistant.

Roy couldn't believe it. He was actually longing for a chit-chat with Brett. *I've really hit the bottom of the toilet bowl.*

He picked up the two-way radio. "How's it going in there?"

"Listening to a show. Singing a few songs. All in all, just dandy. You?"

"I'm freaking dying," Roy admitted. He could hear Brett's laughter through the open companionway.

"I ought to tell your girlfriend that her expensive gift bores you."

"Nothing wrong with the gift. I'm just out of it. These gentle waves aren't helping either."

He heard Brett cut the engine. A few moments later, footsteps echoed through the passageway. Brett emerged on deck and leaned against the starboard side.

Roy shut his eyes. *Well shit. I hoped for a conversation with this guy, and now I'm actually gonna get it.*

Brett wasted no time. "What's the difference between a sailfish and a marlin?"

"Beg your pardon?"

"It's a serious question. I'll say it again: what's the difference between a sailfish and a marlin?"

"You have a Master's degree. You ought to know!"

"Would you just answer the stupid question, please?!"

Roy sighed and slapped his knee. "At least you acknowledge that it's a stupid question. Alright then—Both are members of the billfish family. A sailfish's sail is large and made of accordion pleats. Marlins have a single dorsal fin that connects along the fish's back to a short little ridge. Sailfish tend to average around nine feet and two-hundred twenty pounds, while marlins are way bigger and heavier—fourteen feet and over fifteen-hundred pounds. Sailfins are faster. Good enough?"

"For that, yes," Brett said. "Next question: explain the difference between a colossal and giant squid?"

"Are you for real?"

"Did I stutter?"

Roy groaned. He was tempted to argue, but instead decided to go along with this stupid game. "Colossal squid are larger. The only species that are of the genus Mesonychoteuthis. Giant squids are of Architeuthidae. Their tentacles are longer than the colossal's and their suckers are lined with teeth. The colossal squid's suckers have sharp wheeling hooks. What's the point of this?"

"Why do bull sharks go upriver?"

"Their kidneys recycle the salt within their bodies. They also have glands in their tails that help with salt retention."

"How many fish should we be seeing at this depth?"

"We—" Roy paused. That bastard. Brett Rollins was smarter than Roy cared to give him credit for. He got Roy's brain thinking. Yeah, he knew all the answers, but the little exercise still got the neurons to reactivate, as well as bring his attention to the oddity of what he was seeing on the monitor. Rather, what he was *not* seeing.

"A lot more than this," he said.

"And why's that?" Brett said. "What the hell's going on? Why are we finding a tremendous drop in the fish population, but with no source of the toxins?"

"They're either dying off or—being driven out."

"I don't know about that," Brett said. "It's not like the fish gathered at town hall. 'Hey guys, the toxin levels are elevating. Better move on or we'll all die.' We ought to be seeing a bunch of dead ones."

Roy shook his head. "Except we're not."

"Should we try looking somewhere else?" Brett asked.

"No. I'm bringing it up," Roy said.

"Really? Why? All this time, you were so sure that there'd be something here. There's so much more to search," Brett said.

"I just want to look into something first. Here, you bring the drone up. I'm heading into my office." Roy stood up and entered the companionway, shutting the door behind him. He moved down the small flight of steps and proceeded down the passageway, ultimately finding his work office on the left, right past the main lab.

He took a seat at his desk and started going through his computer files.

All known species of cephalopods.

He scrolled along the index, then clicked on a tab reading *extinct species.*

CHAPTER 17

For the first time in the three hours she was out, Sicilia actually took the time to admire the vessel she stood in. The last time she had operated a boat like this, she was eighteen. Then again, it wasn't this exact vessel, though the one she remembered was almost exactly like it. There weren't quite as many coffee stains on deck as there were on the old boat. The boom was a little wider, and the crow's nest was a few feet higher. Overall, it functioned all the same.

Lucas was there during that final trip. It was as though they knew what her future would hold for the next ten years. Was this her punishment? To return to her only family, only to have him yanked from her life forever? Whatever the case was, this island had lost its sense of beauty in her eyes. Now, it was worse than the prison she felt it to be when growing up. She couldn't look at that thin line in the horizon without thinking of last night's storm. Her uncle's screams were like thunder, echoing in the distance, like he was crying out from the underworld.

Sicilia wondered if the creature was capable of such cries. Was it capable of making any sound at all? Would it cry out when pierced by the hook? Did it smell blood? She didn't know much about cephalopods, let alone an unknown giant species. She knew they were capable of coming up on land, which the one she hunted clearly did.

I hope Uncle Lucas put a bullet through your eye.

She paced back and forth, watching the buoy. The slack in the chain was infuriating. Perhaps it was too shallow. She wondered if the creature would only go for it if it ran deep. It had no problem surfacing last night, but then again, that was at night. Maybe it wanted to avoid the sunlight. Or maybe it just wasn't here to begin with.

Leaning over the guardrail, she studied the deceptively peaceful ocean. Her mind played tricks on her. Every time a cloud would pass overhead and reflect in the mirror-like water, she would hope it was the silhouette of the monster. Instead, all she got was red water.

"Where are you?" Her hands squeezed the guardrail. "Get over here. Come on! COME MEET ME!"

"You talking to us?"

She whipped to her right, almost instinctually going for the shotgun. She was so lost in her trance that she never heard the Coast Guard vessel approach. It was slightly smaller than hers, the hull number reading *45192*. There were two men on board. The one at the cockpit was twenty-one, blonde, and widely alert, while the other…a guy nearing thirty with darker skin and black hair, looked like he'd rather be anywhere else but here.

It was obvious which one asked the question.

"Uh—no," she said.

"Need any help?" the younger one asked.

"I'm fine," Sicilia said. She was trying hard not to come off as angry. Her efforts failed as the questions kept coming. The other guardsman was looking at the chum trail and buoy.

"What's this setup you've got going on?" he asked, inquisitively. "Hunting for sharks?"

"No," Sicilia said. *Take the hint. I'm not interested in chitchat.*

"Looks like a chum trail to me."

"And?" She clamped her jaw shut. Clearly, the one-word answers weren't doing the trick.

"Isn't it illegal to poach for sharks?"

"That's right."

"Then would you mind explaining why you're doing it?"

Sicilia clenched her jaw. Was this guy so bored with his job that he had to bother her? Was this his way of finding amusement? Sicilia was grateful she wasn't standing next to him, because she knew she'd fail to resist the urge to slap him across the face. That, of course, would likely lead to arrest. He seemed the type to arrest people for petty things. Then again, maybe not, as that would likely entail report writing. And this guy didn't seem the type to do any *real* work. Regardless, it took everything to keep herself composed.

"I'm not hunting for sharks," she replied.

The younger one turned to his partner. "Let's just leave her alone."

"Please," she said.

"I'm not sure if we should," the other said.

"Jacob, come on, man!"

The older one scoffed. "*You're* the one who's gung-ho about getting a job done. You see the big hook she's towing? It's no blue shark she's hoping to catch. She's looking for a great white!" He dug out his phone and held it as though ready to snap a video. When he looked back at Sicilia, his expression changed to one of pure glee. "Mind if I get a video?!"

"What?"

"Shut up, Ralf." The older one, Jacob, nodded to Sicilia. "No tricks. I promise. I just want something to entertain me while we're out here."

"I'm not hunting for sharks," Sicilia said.

"Oh really?" Jacob said. "If not sharks, then what?"

Sicilia didn't answer. Last thing she needed was to be called crazy by these two bored guardsmen.

"Just go away, please."

Now Ralf was feeling suspicious. What was this person trying to hide? Still, he wanted to play it diplomatically. Though he didn't have the full details, it was safe to assume she was related to the man who was killed. Then there was the fact that their job was to remain near the island and guard the crime scene.

"My apologies, ma'am," Ralf said. "We noticed you were heading pretty far out. We were worried about you getting out of sight because—"

"I'm not a suspect!" she snapped.

"No-no! I'm talking about those fishermen you warned us about. They might come back and cause trouble. That's why we're over here. We thought *they* might be the group you reported to our Commander." He pointed east. Sicilia looked, seeing a fishing vessel with red paint trawling a quarter-mile out.

"That's not the Glasses," she said. "Their boat is rattier than that."

"Still, we can't keep an eye on you and guard the crime scene at the same time if you go too far out," Jacob said.

Sicilia's patience had worn thin as a microbe. "I'll be able to handle them if they come by. In the meantime, I just want to be left alone. Is that too hard of a concept?"

"I just think it's best—"

"What channel can I reach the Commander on?" She moved to the console and checked the radio frequency. "Twelve, right? Need to warn him about a couple of pricks who won't keep to themselves…"

Ralf felt his whole aviation career come into question. "Okay! Alright. Just PLEASE be careful out here with—" he looked at the buoy and the pinkish piece of meat dangling beneath it— "whatever it is you're doing."

He cut the wheel and took them back toward Diamond Green.

Jacob went over to the cabin. "What do you think she was up to?"

"I thought you didn't care about anything that happened on the job," Ralf said.

"I don't, but I'm also tired of being bored. That lady looks *psycho*!"

"Shh!" Ralf accelerated the vessel. "You're louder than you think."

"Let's dispense with the theatrics. Did Commander Rhea say anything you forgot to relay?"

"No."

"Well, something's not right with that lady."

"She lives on the island. Her family member or companion, whichever he was, had his house torn apart right before he disappeared. She might not be in the best of moods."

"Yeah. So the logical answer is to go out with a big piece of bait on a tri-hook, attached to a chain tied to the rear of a sixty-foot fishing boat. Am I missing something?"

Ralf rolled his eyes. "Unlike you, I'm not looking for things to keep myself occupied."

"That's right. You're here to serve the good ol' red, white, and blue!"

"Nothing wrong with that," Ralf argued. "I'm here to help *protect* that individual, not harass her. Just like the rest of our citizens."

Jacob waited a moment, sincerely hoping that his partner was being intentionally corny. He wasn't. Finally, he broke out in laughter. Ralf turned toward him, his face turning red.

"What's the problem?"

"You're an idealist if there ever was one. Why the hell didn't you join the marines? That's where the real action is."

Ralf sighed. "Pops took issue with it."

"Pops sounds like a smart man," Jacob said. He clasped his hands behind his head and watched the ocean go by. "No sense in risking your neck. Doesn't mean anything at the end of the day."

"Says the guy who goes through life avoiding any challenge coming his way," Ralf replied. "How the hell you've made it this far is beyond me. Actually, scratch that. I know. You're the 'just-enough' guy. Just enough money, just enough effort—just enough to keep you out of trouble."

"Nothing wrong with that. Served me well so far," Jacob said.

After a few minutes, they were near the island. Ralf squinted as he watched the shore. "Where'd it go?"

"Where'd what go?" Jacob said. He was too busy to bother getting a signal on his phone.

"The whale carcass! It's not there anymore," Ralf said. Jacob looked up, then stepped around to the forward deck for a better view. Ralf wasn't exaggerating. The carcass, which had been lying on the sand, had disappeared, leaving a blood-red imprint in the beach where its corpse had been.

"Ooookay," he muttered. "Bizarre, I'll admit." Then he shrugged. "Must've been swept out by the tide.

"I don't think that's what happened," Ralf said.

"No other explanation," Jacob replied. Ralf cut the wheel to the left, then back to starboard, taking them around the south side of the island. Jacob groaned. "Dude, what are you doing?"

"I'm checking your theory. Maybe it drifted off this way. It's not floating to the east. We would've seen it."

"Who's to say it's even floating at all. You see how big those bastards can get. It's probably rolling like a log on the seafloor right now."

"It'd be floating. A whale at that age has enough blubber to help it float. *And* it's been dead for several hours, meaning it's built up a bunch of gas."

"Gas? What, did it eat a bean burrito before dying?" Jacob said with a chuckle.

"No, dipshit. Bacteria goes berserk in their gut, feeding off the tissue and producing gas," Ralf said.

"You read too many books," Jacob said. "That, or you're pursuing the wrong profession."

"At least I'm pursuing *something*," Ralf said. He completed the turn around the tip of the southeast peninsula and gazed out into the ocean. There was nothing but partly cloudy sky and gentle waves before him. No way that whale could have drifted out of sight in the short time they were away. "This is weird." He turned the boat around and took them back near the shore.

"The hell are you doing now?" Jacob said.

"Checking out the beach."

"Dude, you're not a detective."

"The tide didn't rise and fall while we were gone, man," Ralf said. He took the boat into the shallows then aimed his binoculars into the sand. There were a series of strange markings, as though several giant worms had slithered in from the water. "Maybe we should call this in."

"And tell the Commander what?" Jacob said. He raised his fist to his mouth and mimicked a radio call. "Uh, yeah, sir? We've got a missing whale carcass. What do you want us to do about it?"

His tone was ridiculous, but for once he had a point. What would Ralf say? Better to do the explaining afterwards. Still, he felt himself growing antsy. Somewhere off these shores, a boat recently sank. A dock was destroyed. Something ripped into that house. The owner was missing, presumed dead. In the middle of it all, a random whale carcass appeared…only to disappear into thin air, leaving behind strange markings in the sand.

Something weird was going on around here.

****

Sicilia threw another scoopful of chum into the water. She checked the time. It was nearing three-and-a-half hours since she had been out. A feeling of defeat was starting to set in. She dropped the scoop, leaned over the gunwale, and stared out at the world around her. She felt empty and alone. There wasn't a single lifeform in sight, save for the Coast Guard unit, and that fishing vessel they pointed out. She kept an eye on it for a minute. Its hull was red, its length maybe seventy-feet. It did seem to be lingering, but maybe the crew was working on the net. This was a good fishing spot, overall—at least, until the waters were poisoned.

Sicilia turned away. She didn't care who it was, as long as it wasn't the Glasses. This tactic clearly wasn't doing the trick. She didn't know much about cephalopods, whether they could smell blood, or if they hunted in the same manner as sharks.

It certainly has no qualms about coming up to the surface.

Unfortunately, she was no expert fisherman, and had a limited knowledge of ocean life. She had to go with her gut instinct. She was certain that the monster was here somewhere. It just wasn't coming up to the surface. Maybe going deeper was the key. This area was a few hundred feet deep, so she wouldn't have to worry about snagging anything on the seafloor as long as she remained in over fifty-feet of water.

She reeled the chain to the boat. "Alright, Plan B." She detached the buoy and allowed the hook to sink. The chain went taut, the hook dangling like a fishing line below her.

Now at the helm, she turned the boat southeast and engaged the throttle. With the plan in motion, all she had to do was wait for the line to go taut. Then she'd winch the bastard in, point her uncle's shotgun, and deliver retribution.

"Dinner's on the table, you son of a bitch."

CHAPTER 18

Stories of sea monsters is a phenomenon that dates back to the 1500s. Many of these occurrences were documented in the form of Merchant Captain's journals and exaggerated by the imaginations of artists, who depicted the ravenous beasts in paintings and engravings. Many of these cases have remained unproven; many others straight-up refuted as the consequence of storms and waterspouts that haunted voyagers over the centuries.

They have been called many names: Leviathan; Kraken; Lusca; Ningen, and many others. Some were believed to be sea serpents, others to be whales. But none had been captured more in the eye of the population than the giant octopus. Even to this day, stories of sea monsters persist, compounded by the evidence of deep sea life, and the lack of knowledge surrounding many species. And through the years, the reported sightings of enormous cephalopods far outnumbered any other strange beast.

In 1546, a giant squid washed ashore on the coast of what was then Sweden and was reportedly caught while alive. Sketches of the creature were sent by Christian III of Denmark to the Holy Roman Emperor Charles V of Spain. The claim had been disputed over the following centuries, with experts claiming the specimen was unlikely to be a giant squid, but rather a species of shark.

In 1798, on the north coast of Denmark, the body of a giant squid washed ashore and was noted to be large enough to devour ten men. The specimen was then supposedly preserved in a museum in Copenhagen, though few notes had since been made of the creature.

A more interesting story came out of Tasmania, Australia in 1802, where a specimen was reportedly found alive. Stated to be the "size of a barrel" in documents written by the French naturalist Francois Auguste Peron, the creature was described to have "rolled with noise in the midst of the waves, and its long arms outstretched along the surface, and was said to have stirred like so many enormous reptiles."

In 1861, twenty miles northeast of the Canary Islands, officers on the French gunboat *Alecton* reported to have observed the floating corpse of a decomposed specimen. It is believed that the report and sketch made of the specimen was what inspired Jules Verne, who later incorporated the creature into his famous novel *Twenty-Thousand Leagues under the Sea.*

In 1873, near Newfoundland, one was reportedly floating on the surface, when struck by fisherman Theophilus Picot's vessel. The story was titled *A Green-Eyed Monster: The Devil-Fish Seen off the Coast of Newfoundland.* Unsure of what it was they struck and hoping it was something of value, one of Picot's men poked the object with a boat-hook. The author documenting the account described the following incident:

"...Suddenly, the dark heap became animated, and opened out like a huge umbrella without a handle, and the horror-stricken fishermen beheld a face of intelligence, but also ferocity, and a pair of ghastly green eyes glaring at them, its huge parrot-like beak seeming to open with a savage and malignant purpose. The men were petrified with terror, and for a moment so fascinated with the horrible sight that they were powerless."

The author proceeded to describe how the creature lashed out with one of its tentacles, stretching them over the vessel in an attempt to submerge it. Two men were able to sever the tentacle with an axe, driving the creature back into the depths, never to be seen again. The tentacle, described as nineteen feet in length and as thick as a man's wrist, was kept in the city of St. John (Back then, known as St. John's).

Then in May of 1874 came a story of the hundred-and-fifty-ton passenger vessel *Schooner Pearl* which was reportedly sunk by a giant squid. The event was seen by crew of a passenger steamer *Strathowen*, who rescued five of the crew. As with the 1873 Picot incident, it was dismissed as sensational, and ultimately was buried as a fisherman's tale.

Such was the case for the specimen caught in 1875, when Irish fishermen reported to have found a squid floating along the surface, surrounded by seagulls. When attacked, it allegedly sprayed ink and fled. The fishermen claimed to have chased it for five miles before severing its head with a knife.

Up until recently, it was easy for Roy Brinkman to dismiss these reports as imagination gone wild or straight out lies. Now, his opinions wavered. Everything Sicilia said was as fantastical as what these seamen had stated. He hadn't known her long. For all he knew, she was probably a loony. It would be easy to make the case if she was living on this island for several years with little-to-no human contact. Then again, she'd just arrived. And something had come up on the beach. He had seen the markings, which were then fouled by the waves and the rain before the authorities could arrive.

He hadn't had a chance to properly examine the whale carcass yet, but he had seen the injuries. They were not like shark bites. For Commander Rhea, it seemed like an easy matter to assume the whale had raced, maybe blindly, toward the island, thus smashing the dock and sinking the boat. Except there were no marks on its head consistent with such an event. And whatever killed it was strong enough to break its back.

And how did that explain the damage to Lucas Instone's house? Again, the Commander believed it was the Glasses. Fair enough, except why tear down half the building to do it? If they wanted revenge, wouldn't it just be more efficient to go in guns blazing? If they could even obtain weapons to begin with.

The list of unanswered questions only grew longer as Roy turned his eyes to the list of known prehistoric cephalopods.

It all started five-hundred-million years ago, when one-inch long creatures lurked in shallow waters during the Cambrian Era. Fifty-million years later, they began to develop shells, which allowed them to live closer to shore. Soon came the rise of the nautiloids, and the first cephalopods to become predators, the ammonites. Soon, they evolved into coleoids, with shells grown internally, and had evolved with hooks and teeth within their tentacles and the ability to change color.

Most species were very small. The Ectenolites were only a few centimeters in length, as were the shelled Tannuella genus. The Plectronoceras were reported to have only a two-centimeter shell. Only in the Early Ordovician did they start to get a little larger, with shells nearing up to twenty-centimeters in length.

Almost none were considered giant-sized. The largest confirmed extinct specimen was *Tusotheuthis*, which lived during the Cretaceous Period. Roughly the size of a giant squid, it actually was more closely related to present-day octopuses. With its arms outstretched, it was believed to near forty-feet in length. Beyond that, everything else was speculation. Scientists have considered the possibility that other giant cephalopods have existed, though none were ever proven.

Roy clicked on another tab, revealing the sketch of what scientists believed to be an Atlantic Colossal Octopus. During an expedition to the Puerto Rico Trench to collect samples, scientists uncovered what they believed to be a razor-sharp hook, roughly the size of a college textbook. Some researchers believed it to be a shell. What they all agreed upon was that the sample was old and had been broken down by exposure to thermal vents, so it was difficult to determine its origin. Still, sketches were made, comparing the 'hook' to current species of squid. The thought of it belonging to a species of Giant Octopus came full circle with the centuries-worth of tales, when a sixty-foot yacht sank near the Bahamas. When recovered, the yachter described a series of waving serpents with suckers as large as her head. Fragments of the battered hull showed evidence of crushing, even though the vessel was out on the open ocean. Investigators suspected the cause to be a waterspout or rogue wave, or perhaps a rare encounter with a whale. The victim continued the reports of rising tentacles for another week, when suddenly, the story changed to simply, "I was unconscious when the incident occurred. I think I blacked out, because when I regained consciousness, my vessel was going down. My companions were gone. I was alone."

Roy shook his head as he read over the file. "Sounds like she was on the verge of being transferred to an asylum."

He got up, stretched, then entered the storage compartment where the frozen specimens were located. Opening the freezer, he gazed at the creature in stasis. Its skeletal structure, except for the eye sockets, was almost identical to that of the *Materpiscis.*

This creature, which very likely traveled from deeper waters, had been exposed to enormous amounts of dioxin. So much so, that it likely was near the source. Maybe because of an enhanced immune system, it had lasted this long, only to die within the last twenty-four hours.

Roy considered a new possibility: What if there was no waste dump in the nearby vicinity? What if a very large animal was drastically poisoned, its food supply killed off, and driven out of its lair in the depths. In search of new prey, it ventured into shallower waters, while secreting the poison through its skin. A *living* supply of toxin. He thought of the fluctuating levels; particularly how the readings in one area would fall, while readings somewhere else would rise. He had jokingly referred to the scenario as the moving source. Now, he wondered if there was something to it.

Could the consequences of deep water poisoning be even worse than he ever considered? Could something have risen from the abyss?

"Hey, Doc?"

Brett's tone was one of alarm and confusion, not typical of his usual hip personality. Roy hurried to the main deck and joined his assistant at the monitor. The tether was still outstretched, the drone still recording the seabed.

"What's wrong?"

"I decided to play with the drone for a little bit before bringing it up, and—"

"Oh, great. You broke it, didn't you?"

"No, I didn't *break it*!" Brett tapped the joystick to turn the unit around. "No, I was searching around, and I came across *this*."

Roy leaned in as the first object came into view. It was bony white and a few meters long, lined with large teeth. A jawbone, or at least part of one. The camera continued to pan left, revealing curved rib bones, a large rocky structure with an empty socket—a whale skull.

"It's a whale skeleton," Roy said. "Sperm whale, going by that jaw."

"Had to be fifty-feet long," Brett said. More bones came into view. Bits of flesh waved like anemones, appearing white in the drone's spotlight. There was still some dim pink left in the jaw. The state of the flesh suggested it had died recently. "What the hell could do this to a whale?"

Roy leaned away. "Same thing that could sink a boat and tear up a dock."

Brett started to chuckle. "Wait. You think there's a connection between this and what happened to Mr. Instone?"

"Whatever's going on, it isn't normal," Roy said. "This wasn't done by a pod of orcas. And this is the second whale carcass we've come across. Third, if you count the infant that washed up on shore. You saw the humpback yesterday. It had been recently killed. And there's still no trace of the runt."

"There's plenty of explanation for that," Brett said.

"Yeah? Like what? Feeding frenzy? If so, why did it stop? There was plenty of flesh intact to keep a large school of sharks fed for a while. And its flesh was contaminated…"

"Meaning that it ate prey loaded with dioxin," Brett said.

"Or that whatever killed it was the carrier," Roy said. He sighed, watching the screen as more bones came into view. Some had been crushed into jagged fragments. "I think this is the mother of the one that washed up. I think they were attacked. Junior was seized and severely injured. Mom rushed in to protect him, got in a tussle, and ended up here. Meanwhile, Junior died of his wounds and washed up on Diamond Green."

Brett chuckled. "Okay, Detective."

"You have a better explanation?"

"Well, I, uh," Brett cleared his throat, thought for another minute, then looked up at the professor. "You don't *seriously* think this is related to the giant octopus thing?"

"I don't know," Roy said. "But who's to say the paper mill's dumping in the water didn't awaken a monster from the abyss?" Brett opened his mouth to make a sarcastic remark, only to pull back on the reins as he realized the doctor was dead serious.

"Want to keep searching?"

"I think we need to head back," Roy said. "I want to talk with Sicilia again, and wait for the cutter to return. I'd like to convince them to put their advanced sonar to use to see if there's any large objects moving under the surface."

"They'll think you're insane," Brett said.

"You speaking for them? Or for you?" Roy replied.

Brett cleared his throat again. "Noooo. I'd never think you're crazy."

Roy chuckled. "Alright, smartass. Bring the drone up. I'm heading up to the pilothouse."

Brett gave one last glance at the bones. "Hey, doc?"

"Yeah?"

"Random question regarding octopuses and squids: How strong are they, exactly?"

"This one of your 'get me out of brain-fog' questions?"

"Let's say yes," Brett said.

Roy took a deep breath. "Some have been observed lifting forty-times their own body weight. Their bodies rely on a type of skeletal support system called a muscular hydrostat. They have transverse muscle fibers, longitudinal muscle fibers, and helical layers of muscle fibers. Selective activation of these muscle groups allows them to elongate, shorten, bend, tense, and stiffen. Larger species have been known to break the spines of sharks. Might not sound like much considering their skeletons are made of cartilage, but it's actually a deadly feat."

"And if there was a giant octopus as large as what Ms. Instone claims?"

Another deep breath from Roy. "If it closed its arms over this boat like a fist, the *Europa* would look like a soda can in a matter of minutes at best."

Without saying another word, Brett began raising the drone. He looked back at Roy. "Thought you were heading to the pilothouse?"

CHAPTER 19

The chain rattled, then suddenly whipped to the right, sparking Sicilia's attention. This was her third pass, and she was considering on relocating her hunt south of the island. However, it seemed her patience had finally paid off. She stopped the boat and hurried to the winch. The chain continued rattling, like a piece of spider web clinging to an unruly cockroach. Something was on the other end and it was trying desperately to escape.

Her heart thumped like a drum and the tiny hairs on the back of her neck stood on end. The opportunity had struck. She had found her target and was moments away from revenge. The chain swung back and forth, the boat dipping back ever so slightly.

With a pull of the lever, she began reeling the chain in. It came to life with a metallic squeal, then gradually brought the heavy object to the surface. As the length of the chain shortened, it began to extend across the surface as the creature on its hook began to shallow.

Sicilia positioned the shotgun against her shoulder and took aim. She waited for a world of tentacles surrounding the sack-like mantle. She thirsted for blood. Her heart was racing now. Would the shotgun have enough shells to kill it? If not, she had her uncle's revolver strapped over her waist.

Just aim for the eye.

The chain whipped again. A shape began to emerge. Having expected a darker color, she was surprised to see that it was light blue with yellow stripes. Then it broke the surface. A three-foot bill swung back and forth. Its sail sliced the air with a sharp whistling sound.

Sicilia lowered the shotgun. She couldn't believe it. It felt like a sick joke from God Himself! She caught a damn marlin!

She watched the fish crash down into the water. It tried to run, unable to break free of the chain. Shaking with rage, she waited for it to draw near. Twice more, it leapt, still unsuccessful in its attempt to flee. With only fifteen feet to go, she stopped the winch. Her anger boiled, making her feel like a volcano ready to blow its top.

This past twenty-four hours, she had been granted gifts, only to have them yanked away. She was so happy to return to her childhood home, only to see that the reefs she explored as a kid were quickly dying. She was reunited with her beloved uncle, only to hear him be taken to his death by a ruthless monster. She found what she felt was new love, only to piss that away with her lust for vengeance. And to top it off, that vengeance she so desperately craved looked as though it was going to be paid off, but it was all a mirage. A sick tease after hours of nothingness.

Exhaustion from stress, anger, and lack of sleep were taking its toll. If Sicilia's mind could exert physical force, the whole ocean would be raised in a catastrophic waterspout. But alas, she was a powerless human with nothing else left in the world except her anger. She had been used, mistreated, assaulted, and put down by the world. Now nature was adding to the fray, with this piece-of-shit marlin tricking her into believing it was the beast that took her uncle.

Sicilia aimed her weapon at the fish. If she couldn't get revenge for Lucas' death then at least she should get something for this trickery. She slid her finger over the trigger and slowly began applying pressure. The muzzle shook. She watched the fish jerk back and forth, blood seeping from where the hook was embedded in its mouth.

Sweat accumulated on her forehead. She applied a little more pressure. Another millimeter and she would feel the recoil. Yet, she couldn't do it. It was like there was a cinder block keeping the trigger from going back any further.

With a gasp, she lowered the weapon, then fell to her knees. She threw her face into her palms and wept. This wasn't her. She was no murderer, even of animals. Her mind briefly tried to justify her near-actions, but she quickly shot them down. No, this wasn't the same thing as fishing. There was no sport in this. The marlin didn't have malice. It was just trying to survive in a dying ocean, and took a chance on a piece of meat. It had no concept of her grief.

For several minutes, she continued weeping, apologizing to her uncle in Heaven for her bad deed. It was a powerful release, a lifting of the spirit. It didn't take away any of the pain, but it did help. The weeping ceased, leaving Sicilia leaning against the transom exhausted. She would've been tempted to fall asleep if the fish didn't keep splashing water over her.

"Alright, I get it," she said to the marlin. "I won't kill you. I *ought* to use you as bait, little fucker. But I won't."

The fish slowed, having spent much of its energy. It moved back and forth, like a bass on a stringer. She examined the placement of the hook to see if there was a way she would be able to get it out. There would be no way of doing so without hauling the fish on board. She still had her father's nets. All she would have to do is get one around it, raise the thing out of the water, and pry the hook out. It'd leave a nasty little sore, but it was better than death.

"Hey-hey! Take a look at this!" a voice cried out from behind her. Sicilia froze.

"Oh, shit." She slowly turned. That red fishing vessel was approaching. Had she not been preoccupied, she would have heard it approach. She wiped her eyes and hoped that it wasn't too obvious she was crying. Then again, she didn't care that much.

On the flybridge was a man in his early fifties, wearing an open white shirt and a battered ball cap whose bill was frayed all along the rim. Whomever he was talking to, they were either below deck or on the main deck behind the structure, where she couldn't see. *Great. Another group of idiots who can't keep to themselves. Didn't I come to this island to get AWAY from people?*

"Looks like you've won yourself a trophy!" the man said.

Sicilia decided to play along. "Sometimes luck is in your corner."

"Not quite the usual setup for marlin fishing you've got going on there," he said.

"I decided to improvise," she replied. The man turned his vessel to starboard, aligning it with hers. Though only slightly longer than her father's boat, the structure towered high above hers, making this stranger's vessel appear almost gargantuan. She had to really cock her head back to look her visitor in the eye. She couldn't help but notice that nobody was on the main deck still. Even more odd; the nets didn't look wet. Had they even touched the water? Hell, they didn't even look baited. What was this guy doing all the way out here if he wasn't trawling?

"Looks like it worked out well for ya," the man said.

"Perhaps," Sicilia said. She was getting nervous. Something about this visit didn't seem right. She started inching her way to the cockpit. "Just got lucky, I guess."

"Yeah, me too," the guy said.

"How so?" Sicilia asked. She reached the ladder.

"Well, I saw the visitors you had recently," he said. "I appreciate you turning them away. Makes things *much* easier."

Her eyes widened. Instinctively, her hand inched for the revolver at her waist. She heard a splash near the port bow, followed by a high-pitched *cling*. Sicilia hurried across the side-deck, then stopped. Pulling against the guardrail was a tri-hook. The stem angled backward, pulled by the rope that was fastened through the eye. Before Sicilia could react, Mel Glass hauled himself aboard. In his hand was his speargun, loaded and ready to fire.

Dripping wet, he looked—and smelled—like he just swam through a pipeline. He turned toward Sicilia and greeted her with his broken-toothed smile. "Hi, Missy! I see you met my nephew, Ricky!"

Dawn quickly climbed up behind him. Her face was riddled with cuts and bruises, which only added to her natural demonic facial expression. The two of them had actually swum across while her attention was on the guy named Ricky.

Sicilia stumbled backward. What was she thinking making the Coast Guard guys go away? She would have to handle this situation *herself* now. Her fingers closed over the grip of her revolver. She heard a sharp *whoosh* and felt the breeze of a rigid object shooting an inch away from her face. Glancing back to the large red vessel, she saw the nephew, Ricky's, first mate. He was a large, burly man. He had tossed away the speargun and scooped up another, which was already loaded. Meanwhile, Ricky cackled as he pointed a bolt-action rifle at her.

"I'd appreciate if we could do this quietly," he said.

Sicilia trembled. "Do *what*?"

Mel began to laugh. Even from twelve feet away, she could smell the alcohol. That speargun remained pointed at her midsection. Dawn stepped around him. She didn't hold any projectile-weapons, though there was a large knife tucked in her belt.

"Don't make a move for that six-shooter," she said. "Ricky's mate, Stone, he's a good shot. Only reason he missed you the first time was because he's a courteous fellow. He's from Colombia—used to enforce for Chavez before the CIA took him down…in favor of Ramos the Jackal."

Sicilia backed up until her back was against the structure. What has this world become?! This place used to be a paradise. She used to think of it as one of God's gardens. Now, it was a place of death, poison, beasts, and murderers. Not only was she in a faceoff against two crazed fishermen, but now also their equally-crazed nephew and his cartel-enforcer, Stone. Hell, no wonder those nets didn't seem used—Ricky probably made his money shipping drugs.

There was no use in pleading for mercy. Beyond being crazy as hell, these peoples' brains were fouled by alcohol, and probably drugs. Her only chance of escape would be to rely on herself.

"Where's your doctor friend?"

"Don't know," she said.

"I smell bullshit," Dawn said.

"Me too," Mel replied.

"Sure that's not just your own natural scent?" Sicilia said. The crazed couple simultaneously broke out in laughter.

"Very funny. Let's see how you laugh. I'm sure we'll get a few good squeals out of you while we wait for the doc."

Sicilia took the chance. She lunged to her left and dropped below the gunwale. Both Mel and Stone fired their spears, each whizzing over their target and striking wood and glass. Hearing the sound of the spear punching through her windshield, Sicilia knew they had missed. She then sprinted to the main deck, closely followed by the Glasses. As they followed her, the henchman Stone rushed to the foredeck of Ricky's vessel, while loading his speargun. Even now, they were determined to do this silently.

With only a moment to react, Sicilia drew her uncle's revolver. In that split-second, she debated whether to fire it at the Glasses or at their companions. She chose the people with the projectile weapons. Gripping the weapon with both hands, she squeezed off a shot at Stone. The bullet missed, but did cause him to dive for cover. Instead of wasting another shot on him, she pointed the weapon at Ricky. Again, she missed, but it wasn't all for nothing, as her shot caused *him* to miss as well. The .308 round, which had been aimed at her chest, struck the deck at her feet while he jerked to the side to avoid her shot.

It was a struggle for Sicilia to keep control of the weapon. With each shot, it threatened to leap from her grip. Worse yet, the Glasses were coming at her in full sprints. Sicilia pivoted on her heel and fired blindly at the duo. Miraculously, the shot hit one of the targets. A cloud of pink exploded from Mel's shoulder, causing him to spin to his left, right into Dawn. The knife was drawn now. The insane woman pushed her injured husband out of the way and slashed wildly at Sicilia.

She screamed, throwing both hands over her face. The blade struck the muzzle of her revolver and knocked it from her grip. Sicilia dove to her right and grabbed the shotgun, only to have it kicked away by Dawn. The next kick connected with her stomach.

Dawn knelt beside her, grabbed a fistful of hair, and pulled Sicilia's face toward hers. "Now you've really done it, you little bitch." Sicilia grimaced. The only thing worse than the pain and terror was the vile smell. Until now, she only thought buried corpses could smell this bad. She looked past Dawn at Mel, who picked up her revolver from the deck. His wife smiled maniacally. "You have a lot of repaying to do. I'll let Mel, Ricky, and Stone decide what to do. More specifically; who goes first."

"Oh, there's no deciding," Mel said. He tucked the revolver in his pocket and reached for his fly. Panic gripped Sicilia's mind. All of her life she avoided cities and slums, mostly out of fear of some rapist battering down her door. She never considered the possibility that such a thing would occur *here*. She yelled out and threw a fist into Dawn's jaw, knocking her back. Springing to her feet, Sicilia tried to make a run for the ladder, but Mel had already lunged for her. He slammed her against the gunwale. Once again, he had the revolver in hand and pointed right at her chin.

Up close, he smelled even worse than his wife. His eyes were red and veiny, his skin oily despite having recently submerged in water. Blood trickled from the flesh wound in his shoulder.

"You've done pissed me off," he said. "Get on your knees."

"Fuck you," Sicilia spat.

He pressed the muzzle to her closed lips. "One way or another, you'll be sucking on something. The fact that I'm letting you choose which is a courtesy." He started digging the muzzle into her mouth. Sicilia whipped her head back and forth, while the rest of the gang proceeded to laugh at her misery.

"Hurry it up, Uncle Mel," Ricky said.

"Patience!" Mel called back.

Ricky paced up on the deck of his vessel, amused but also impatient. He was hot and eager for his turn, especially since the wench dared fire a shot at him. There was no empathy for the fact that she acted out of self-defense. It was only his desires that mattered, no matter the surrounding circumstance. As he waited, he picked up his rifle from the deck, then stood watch. He kept his eyes on the island. So far, it didn't seem that the Coast Guard fellas had heard the shots, otherwise, they'd be speeding to the rescue.

"What's that?" Stone said. He pointed to the water behind Sicilia's vessel. Ricky looked, seeing nothing but water and the marlin now going crazy. It twisted about, tugging on the chain and splashing water with its tail.

"Just a fish, you idiot," he replied.

"No. I thought I saw something else," Stone said. "Under the water."

Ricky looked for a second, failing to see anything. He turned his eyes to his first mate and chuckled. "You're just so anxious to have the woman that you're seeing things." Stone didn't reply. Instead, he pointed again, then jumped back. Ricky looked again. This time, his grin faded. It was like looking at an enormous thundercloud. Its black shape expanded like an umbrella, with serpent-like shapes stretching toward the surface.

The marlin was snatched and pulled to the depths, dragging the chain and everything attached to it.

Sicilia was on the verge of accepting her fate when suddenly the boat lurched backward. Mel stumbled backwards and fell, as did Dawn, who nearly flipped over the transom. The boat seemed to race backward all on its own. Waves of water surged onto the deck with tremendous force, knocking Dawn flat on her back.

People and equipment washed about. Sicilia clung to a metal cleat on the inner starboard gunwale, which kept herself from falling. She watched the ocean rise to the edge of the transom, ready to spill freely and sink them to their doom.

With a high-pitched *snap* the chain broke. The boat righted itself, nearly catapulting Sicilia, who continued to hold herself in place. The Glasses rolled about, alarmed and confused. The boat was now a few hundred feet away from Ricky, who started his engine back up.

"What the hell was that?" Mel shouted. Sicilia couldn't believe it. This psychopath was asking *her*, as though nothing sinister had been taking place in the preceding moments. Nope, just a bunch of friends hanging out.

She felt something bump her foot. She glanced down and realized it was her speargun. Mel noticed it too, and started to raise his revolver. Sicilia dropped to her knees, picked up the weapon, and squeezed the trigger. The projectile whizzed by Mel's cheek, grazing it. The fisherman spun about. He touched his cheek, looked at the blood on his hand, then smiled. It was relief and amusement all in one.

He looked back toward his victim. "Not a very good shot, are ya?" He pointed the revolver and began to squeeze the trigger.

The ocean erupted behind him. Rising high was a sucker-lined tentacle, looking like a mythical sea serpent as it coiled ten feet over its target. Little brown-colored teeth protruded from the lines of each sucker. Behind it, the water bulged, then broke apart, revealing the rounded body the arm was connected to. Two enormous eyes opened, their purple glow dim in the sunlight.

As though shot through spring-loaded force, the tentacle lashed at Mel and coiled around him like a python. His arms, pinned against his body, were the first to snap. His ribs and spine broke loudly in the following instant, causing blood to spurt from his mouth, ears, and wherever bone fragments protruded from his body. Then he was lifted from the deck and hauled into the water, under the beast, and vanished with an audible *crunch*.

The clouding of blood left little to the imagination of what occurred. Mel was gone, leaving behind no trace, except for the dropped revolver. Dawn froze in place. One second her husband was there. The next, he wasn't. She wondered if she was lost in some strange hallucination. It had been twelve hours since they consumed the mushrooms.

The wet, leathery feeling of the next tentacle reaching over the transom snapped her back into reality. By then, it was too late. It looped around her waist and squeezed, driving the razor-sharp teeth into her flesh. Blood sprayed like sprinkler water. Dawn screamed and writhed. Though she had the knife in her hand, she was in too much agony to actually consider using it against the beast.

Sicilia dropped the speargun and staggered backward, watching as Dawn was pulled over the side. The tentacle whipped her about as would a child playing with his food. Finally, she disappeared under a splash of red water. There was another *crunch*, followed by the brief grinding of flesh and bone.

More tentacles slithered their way on deck. Sicilia hyperventilated. It was true. Her imagination hadn't played tricks on her. The monster was real. And now, she realized what a fool she was for going after it. Now, three of its eight arms were sliding toward her. The beast understood that boats carried humans. It knew how to catch them. To it, she was nothing more than a piece of protein.

The boat started tilting back again. She could hear the scraping of tentacles against the keel. It was about to pull the whole boat down—but not before snatching the human aboard.

Her heel hit something. The shotgun! Sicilia grabbed it, pointed at the nearest tentacle, and squeezed off a shot. A gaping hole exploded in the eighteen-inch-wide appendage, which immediately rolled backward. She pumped the shotgun and fired at the next tentacle. More flesh shot across the deck.

The beast retracted, the vessel rocking as it was freed from its grasp.

It did feel pain. Such knowledge brought with it a feeling of satisfaction. But it didn't blind Sicilia to the danger she was still in. The beast had simply flinched and lost its grip. She only had seconds before it would attack again.

She grabbed the revolver, tucked it in its holster, and climbed onto the flybridge. With a push of the throttle, she launched the boat forward.

"Shit!" she exclaimed. Ricky's vessel was right in her path, making a turn to port after he saw the leviathan in the flesh. Sicilia spun the wheel to starboard, narrowly avoiding contact with their hull.

Yet, there was still impact, not in front, but from underneath. She hit the deck as her boat spun like a top along the surface. Tentacles rose up on each side, light-red in color, smelling absolutely horrid. They lashed about like whips, crumpling the hull. She could hear the keel being crushed and felt the vibrations under her feet. Still determined to fight, she aimed the shotgun down at the waving appendages and fired. Her aim had improved drastically in the last five minutes, as had her handling of weapons in general. Then again, she had larger targets to shoot at, and much more hate to bring her focus.

There was a muffled groan from under the water. The creature *could* make sound. It was yelling out in pain. Good. All the more reason to shoot it again. She watched the flesh explode from the next shotgun blast. Once again, the creature retracted, allowing her to throttle at full-speed.

Driven by jet propulsion, the beast followed. From high above, it looked like a red cloud moving under the water. Its tentacles separated as it sucked in more water, then shot back directly behind it as it expelled the load. Water surged directly above it, like a force field surrounding a futuristic space vessel. Its eyes were like telescopes, zooming in on each of the targets above. It saw two boats, one somewhat larger than the other. The creature's brain rationalized that the larger vessel naturally held more lifeforms for it to snatch. Also, the other was damaged and moving more slowly, while the larger was able to continue at full speed.

It was simple logic to take down the stronger vessel before it escaped, then turn its focus onto the damaged one after. The creature absorbed thousands of gallons of water, then spat it out, launching its enormous body like a rocket. It passed underneath the red vessel. With one more blast of water, it was ahead of it.

It broke the surface, hissing like a snake, while thrusting its many arms at the hull.

Ricky screamed. The red mantle seemed to appear out of nowhere. Though soft and fleshy, it also had a rigid appearance. Razor-sharp spines protruded from the top and back. A sickening suctioning sound filled the air, reminding him of the drain in his kitchen.

Tentacles whipped about like kite strings, crushing the guardrail, splintering decking, ultimately squeezing the bow together. Tentacles lapped over the front of the boat and squeezed like a fist. Pressure mounted, ultimately rupturing the hull. Pieces of deck popped like champagne corks. The creature's sick, rotting smell combined with the odor of diesel fuel and oil. Smoke spat from the engine and twisted high into the sky, carrying the smell of fumes with it.

****

"Doc?! HEY! DOC! You see this?!"

Roy hurried out onto the deck and saw his assistant pointing to the north. There, they saw the large trail of smoke against the blue sky. Below it were two boats, maybe a half-mile away. It was too hard to see exactly what was going on, but it was common sense to know it wasn't good.

"Sweet Jesus. Let's get over there." Roy hurried to the pilothouse. He pointed the boat at the incident and accelerated to top speed.

****

The creature proceeded to pull the bow into the water. The sudden shift threw Ricky against the console. He fumbled to keep his grip on the rifle, which nearly slid over the controls and off the flybridge out of reach. He caught it by the grip, then placed a foot on the edge of the console to help balance himself against the vessel's downward slope. He took aim at the writhing mass in front of him. Not that he really needed to aim—the thing had to be at least ninety-feet from the back of its mantle to the tips of its outstretched tentacles.

He fired a shot into its head. The beast gave a mild jolt, as though the bullet was the equivalent of a needle prick. It didn't give any impression that it was injured. Ricky chambered another round and fired again.

A shadow overtook him. He looked up, then quivered at the sight of the tentacle stretching ten feet above him. His bullets did little to harm the beast, but a lot to *annoy* it. He threw his arms over his eyes and screamed. The tentacle snatched him by the legs and hoisted him into the air upside down. Ricky dangled, losing the rifle in the process, and simply flapped about like a worm caught in a bird's beak.

His shins were compressed, the teeth of the suckers cutting through his pantlegs. He could feel the pressure mounting to the breaking point.

"No-no-no! Stop-stop-stop!!!"

SNAP!

Ricky screamed in agony. Dangling by two broken legs, he writhed, swinging like a pinata. The tentacle continued to squeeze further, this time snapping the femurs as it carried him to its 'master'. Ricky saw the purple eye of the cephalopod staring at him briefly before leaning back to reveal its mouth. Ricky gasped—then gagged after unintentionally inhaling the foul odor. The front tentacles and the webbing between them peeled back like onion layers, revealing the fleshy white underside. A membrane material unveiled like eyelids, and a huge eagle-like beak protruded. It opened wide, exposing a tongue lined with razor teeth. Like a ninth tentacle, it slithered along the lower jaw, ready to grind the prey into minced meat.

Another sludging sound filled Ricky's ears as hot air filled his nostrils; the last thing his senses would register. That, and the sensation of being grounded into pulp.

Stone watched the red water billow from under the beast. His Captain was gone. He made his way to the stern of the vessel, which was now the only part of the boat above water. The ocean had consumed the entire bow, and the other half was quickly following. He held his spear gun in one hand and a machete in the other. Bare chested, scar-faced, and armed with blades, he resembled a warrior from fairy tales, ready to take on the immense beast.

However, his last stand wouldn't be so epic. The tentacles moved faster than he did, and before he could take aim, the speargun was ripped from his grasp—along with his right arm. All he felt was a brief tug. Only when he saw the blood spurting from the stub did he realize what had happened. Determined to go out fighting, he slashed the machete. There was no technique or aim, he just went wild as his vision blurred.

Like several individual entities, the tentacles lunged at once. One gripped him by the remaining arm, another by the waist, and a third looped under the shoulders. Simultaneously, they pulled him apart. Organs fell to the deck, painting it red, only to be washed away moments later by the ocean.

The monster feasted on the individual body parts, savoring the taste of this newly-discovered meal that typically dwelled on land. There was more to be had. The monster pushed itself away from the sunken boat. Its sensory organs detected movements from the damaged vessel, which was a few hundred yards away, but moving slowly.

It filled itself with a thousand gallons of water and expelled it. Like a deflating balloon, the beast shot through the water, quickly closing the distance on its next meal.

CHAPTER 20

Sicilia looked over her left shoulder just in time to witness Ricky's boat disappear beneath the waves. What frightened her more than that horrendous sight was the reddish 'cloud' moving like a bullet under the water. It stopped, expanded once, then squeezed itself to expel the water it had absorbed.

She turned her eyes forward. She could see the island now. Maybe fifteen-hundred yards. Too far. She looked back to the creature, just in time to see it close the distance. Its mantle struck the port quarter. The vessel fishtailed like a car on an icy lot.

Sicilia ducked and pressed herself to the helm to keep from hitting her head. The beast initiated its assault. Tentacles whipped at the boat. It remembered the harm she inflicted on it, thus, it had no intention of taking its sweet time. The arms splintered the deck, pulled the guardrail apart, and tore at sections of the gunwale. One arm grabbed the crow's nest and waved it like a flag before tossing it aside.

The beast pressed its body to the hull. Its beak extended, opened wide, and closed down on the keel, piercing the metal as easily as though it were made of cardboard.

It whipped the boat around effortlessly, rocking its operator to-and-fro. Twice, Sicilia failed to aim with the shotgun. There was no way she could release her grip on the wheel without being tossed about.

One of the arms slithered up to the flybridge, its rounded tip pointing at her as it curled around the rim. Though it had no eyes, it looked as though it 'saw' her. Sicilia shrieked. She pointed the shotgun with one hand and squeezed the trigger. The weapon rocketed from her grasp and flipped end over end before hitting the water. The shot wasn't for naught, however. The buckshot erupted the tip of the tentacle. It whipped out of sight, buying her a few moments to stand back up.

When Sicilia looked at her father's boat, she saw something that looked entirely different than the vessel she boarded hours earlier. The structure was being crushed, the deck ripped out, the engine and cargo hold exposed, spewing smoke and vapor around her. And doing the devious work was the beast, who was now raising its body up along the portside. Its humongous eyes gazed at her, the spiny mantle behind them pulsating.

Fear took a paralyzing hold. Her throat tightened as though constricted by one of those horrible tentacles. She looked back at the island, the sight of which now seemed like a mean-spirited tease.

A droning sound drew her attention to the south. A boat horn. She looked past the creature and spotted Roy Brinkman's vessel speeding toward her. It was about a thousand feet away and coming in fast. Brett was waving at her from the bow rail.

They wouldn't be able to get close with the beast…

Sicilia spat, freeing herself from fear's grip, and drew the revolver. She cranked the lever back until it locked, then rested her arms over the guardrail, steadying her aim on the creature's right eye.

Droplets of blood squirted from the corner of its eye as the bullet punched through. All eight tentacles coiled back. The beast reeled backward, its tentacles instinctively gathering over its head.

The *Europa* came in along the starboard side. "Come on! It's coming back!"

Roy opened the cockpit window. "Si! You'll have to jump!"

She was way ahead of him. She propped her foot over the guard rail. There was brief hesitation. Even in this circumstance, leaping across boats, with a ten-plus foot drop was a daunting task. Only when she heard the creature breach the water behind her did she commit to it.

She hit the deck, feeling something pop in her ankle. She yelped, but continued to move across the deck to get as far away from the predator as possible.

"Good God!" Brett shouted. The beast continued its assault on Sicilia's boat, crushing it like a Styrofoam cup.

Roy pointed the *Europa* toward Diamond Green and pushed the engine to its maximum capability. Sicilia hurried inside and embraced Roy.

"Oh, Jesus! Thank God you showed up."

He kissed her on the head, then looked at the creature. "My God, you were right. I should've listened to you."

She put a hand on his shoulder. He could feel it shaking with adrenaline. "It's okay, Roy. Just get us on dry land."

"Hey, guys?!" Brett shouted from outside. "I think it's coming after us."

They both looked back again. The creature had cracked the vessel in two, the bow and stern both pointing upward into a V-shape. Both halves drifted away from each other as a gargantuan force passed between them. Large swells rolled over the creature, with jets of water streaming behind it.

"Fuck me," Roy said. He grabbed the radio mic and switched it to Twelve. "Coast Guard, Coast Guard, this is Professor Roy Brinkman of the *Europa*. Come in, over." He tapped his hand nervously against the helm.

"This is Commander Rhea. Go ahead, Doctor."

"Commander, I know this'll sound crazy, but we are being pursued by a large organism. A cephalopod of some kind. It sank Sicilia Instone's vessel and is now coming after us. We are less than a half-mile east of Diamond Green, but it's closing in. We need help right away."

Moments passed. He could imagine the Commander's face. The guy was probably questioning whether the doctor had gone insane.

"45192, do you copy?"

"Willis here. I copy, Commander. Turning thirty-degrees port to intercept."

"You have guns on that boat, Ensign?" Roy asked.

"Affirmative."

"Good. Lock and load. You'll understand in a minute."

****

"What the hell? Is this world really going insane?" Jacob said.

"Apparently so," Ralf Willis replied.

"You actually believe this shit about a giant sea monster?" Jacob said.

"Chriiiiist," Ralf moaned. He turned to his companion. "Take the damn helm. *I'll* prep the gun."

"Fine by me," Jacob said. Driving was no big deal. Let the gung-ho commando wannabe fire the M240 Bravo. In the rare occurrence the weapon was used, there was usually mountains of paperwork to be filled out, not to mention the inventory of the rounds used. Yep, driving the boat was definitely the right option for Jacob Anthony.

Ralf mounted the machine gun on the foredeck and placed his aviators over his eyes to protect them from the wind. He could see the *Europa* moving toward him. There was only about seven-hundred yards of distance, which was shrinking fast.

"I don't see any sea monster," Jacob said.

"Shut up, man," Ralf said. He noticed the *Europa* showed no signs of slowing down. It was making a straight line for the island, with no intent on stopping for them.

"It dove! Watch yourselves. It could be anywhere now," the civilian said through the radio.

"Uh-huh. *Of course* it did—JESUS CHRIST!!!" The way the ocean erupted behind the *Europa*, it was as though a bomb had detonated directly under the surface. However, this thing was worse than explosives; it was a living, breathing, shipwrecking, kraken-like monster.

It reached out with its arms, each one a destructive menace determined to wreak havoc on anything they touched. Four of them grabbed ahold of the *Europa*, halting it in place. Water sprayed in all directions. There was a brief fountain of red that jetted out from the starboard side. The monster released its grip and dove, having been nicked by one of the propellors.

The *Europa* was moving again. It crossed another couple of hundred feet before the large shape emerged again. This time, it came up along the starboard side. Its arms, some dripping blood, thrashed the boat like bullwhips. Some grabbed ahold on the structure and gunwale, and began to pull. The boat leaned to starboard.

Both guardsmen looked to each other, each checking their own sanity. Jacob resisted the urge to turn the boat around. "That gun is loaded, right?"

Ralf tugged on the cocking lever. "Let's do this!" He took a deep breath, aimed the weapon, then unleashed its fury on the creature. Bits of flesh popped from its mantle as the bullets struck. Blood filled the surrounding water. "Come get some!"

"Keep at it," a nervous Jacob said. There was visible damage to the creature. It wasn't invincible. It bled and it was in visible pain. All they had to do was put enough lead into its body.

The creature released its grip on the boat and thrashed its arms about. It was in pain, but couldn't immediately sense where the assault was coming from. All it could comprehend was that it was coming from the surface. It rolled its enormous bulk and submerged, leaving rolling waves of frothing water behind.

****

Roy clung tightly to the helm to keep from falling as the *Europa* rocked to port and back. They were moving again, though a little more sluggishly. The sound of clunking metal within the engine made his heart jump. A few seconds ago, he considered making a Hail Mary attempt to reach the mainland. Considering the creature's ability to come on land and its ability to tear the side of a house open, there was little safety in taking refuge on Diamond Green. But now, there was no choice. The *Europa* would not survive the trip.

"You alright?" he asked Sicilia. She nodded. He then grabbed the radio. "Thanks, boys. You saved our asses. Watch out, the thing knows you're a threat and will come for you next. It might strike from underneath."

"We hit it pretty hard. It might be dead or dying."

"I saw the way it dove. It was evading. Watch out. It'll probably strike again."

****

Ralf swung the weapon around, searching for any unusual shape under the water. "What? You a pussy? Come on, squiddy."

Jacob, on the other hand, wasn't feeling as enthusiastic. "Let's head for shore."

"Man up, dude," Ralf said. Jacob didn't appreciate the remark. The guy was six years younger than him. Perhaps he saw his feistiness as having bigger balls, but Jacob saw his desire to flee as a sign of more common sense.

"I don't see it," Jacob said. He waited a few more seconds. "Fuck it. I'm taking us to shore."

"Wait, man!"

"Nope. Not waiting!" Jacob spun the wheel, completing a wide turn until the bow was facing the island. A few more moments, and they'd be on dry land…

Like angry sea serpents, the tentacles burst from the water and rose above the stern. Jacob turned around just in time to see the leathery arms lash out at him. They coiled around his midsection and dug their teeth into his ribs. He arched back and screamed.

In the midst of his terror and pain came the agonizing thought: had he just kept the boat facing east and took the fight to the creature, it would've surfaced in front of them, allowing Ralf to gun it down. Instead, he allowed his cowardice to get in the way.

The tentacle tripled the pressure, crunching his ribs and driving them into his lungs, rupturing his insides. His scream ceased as a gushing scarlet fountain erupted from his mouth. His insides sprayed the deck as he was pulled into the water and into the jaws of the beast. The beak and razor tongue only needed three-seconds to turn him into mulch.

By the time Ralf pointed the gun to the rear, his teammate was gone. Even worse, he couldn't get a clear shot at the creature.

"Shit! SHIT!!!" He turned it to the left and fired a few bursts at a tentacle that waved to the side. The sting of the bullet striking its flesh enraged the beast further. All eight of them went to work, wrapping around the vessel and crushing it. The engine clunked then burst into pieces, while everything else imploded.

The tentacles covered everything except a couple of feet of the forward deck, where Ralf stood. There was no choice. He had to jump and take his chances.

He leapt face-first off the boat and was stroking as soon as he touched the water. Now, all thoughts of bravery patriotism were out the window. Gasping in horror, he chastised himself. Had he simply allowed Jacob to turn back when he initially wanted to, he'd be on land right now. But no, he had to prove to the world how brave he was.

He felt the leathery touch of one of the arms on his legs. In the blink of an eye, he was yanked under the water. It didn't bother crushing him before offering him to the quick, but excruciating fate of being put through the organic equivalent of a woodchipper.

The creature extended its tongue and gorged. It wasn't done. The large vessel was still in the water. Though injured in the recent skirmish, its need to kill was insatiable. It couldn't let this enemy escape.

It pointed its mantle north and resumed the chase.

****

"Oh my God," Sicilia said, cupping a hand over her mouth. Brett ran into the pilothouse.

"Boss, it's coming again."

Roy looked out the window, seeing the swells pushed aside by the advancing beast. The Coast Guard boat was wrecked, its personnel dead. With the cutter out of the area, they were defenseless.

"Shit." He tried to think of a solution. Taking a glance at the cove as they cleared the peninsula, a thought came to mind. It'd be a longshot, and it'd probably get him killed, but then again, that fate was looking more likely with each passing moment.

He steered the boat toward the dock. "Get out! Hurry! Hurry! Hurry!" He slowed, only to keep from ramming into the dock itself. "Go! Jump!"

"Wait! What about you?" Sicilia asked.

"I'll be fine. I've got a plan. It'll only work if you leave *now*!" Roy said. Sicilia pressed her lips to his, then followed Brett onto the deck. They leapt from the starboard bow into the water near the dock. As they swam the couple of yards to the dock, Roy pointed the vessel south and pushed it again at full speed.

With the boat now on autopilot, he hustled into the lower decks. He found his diving gear, a couple of knives, a scuba tank, and, most importantly, his diver propulsion vehicle. When he arrived on the upper deck, he heard water cresting over the forward bow. By the time the sunlight touched his forehead, the creature had arrived.

Tentacles immediately went to work wrecking the ship. The radio antenna was the first to go, along with a large section of the pilothouse. Two of the front arms stretched across the main deck, tilting the *Europa* to port as the beast hauled itself aboard.

Roy could see its rounded mantle. It was coated with spines like those from desert spiders and insects protruding outward. There were small patches of white where the Coast Guard patrollers had shot it, though he couldn't gauge how critical the injuries were—considering that the boat was coming apart. He had seconds before those eyes would emerge. He threw the tank, rebreather, and goggles on, then dove off the starboard side. After sinking a few feet, he activated the diver propulsion vehicle and pointed himself toward the island. He had a little less than a thousand feet to go. With the *Europa* still moving south with the monster riding its deck, his chances were good.

It didn't leap into the water after him. So far, it still thought the pesky humans were inside the boat.

He kicked his feet to increase speed. He regretted not having flippers, which would certainly help. His chances were improving though. The seafloor beneath him contained recognizable elements during his many dives. The flower-shaped patch of coral, the twin brain coral that had an alien look to it—he was almost there.

With the help of the device, he cleared the distance in two minutes. He surfaced ten feet from the edge of the dock. Tossing the device aside, he paddled the rest of the way, hauled himself out of the water, then ran for the hill.

"Roy!"

He threw the foggy goggles off. With his vision cleared, he realized Sicilia was standing by the front door. She never went in, as she couldn't stand the thought of abandoning him. Brett, on the other hand, had no qualms about hiding.

Roy reached the top of the hill and embraced her in a hug. He looked out into the ocean in time to see his research vessel break apart. The creature had broken the bow clean off the rest of the boat and was lifting it clear over its head. It slammed it down, resulting in a huge splash, then proceeded to peel the hull from the rest of the vessel. It was confused and frustrated, having failed to find any tasty humans in the boat.

"Get inside," Roy said. They shut the door behind them and locked it. Together, they glared at the puny door-lock, then glanced through the window at the wrecked boat.

"Don't think that's gonna do us much good," Sicilia admitted.

"Yeah…" Roy muttered. "Still… let's barricade this place. Maybe if we block out the windows, it won't see us. Brett?! Where the hell are you?"

They heard feet coming down the stairs. "Oh, thank God. Doc, I thought you were dead."

"No, but there is some bad news—that thing sank your hot pockets."

"Even *worse!*" Brett managed to laugh at his own joke, though it was all a façade. One of the reasons he was quick to go upstairs was to use the bathroom. During the whole chase, he had to clamp down, or else be humiliated before dying a horrible death.

Sicilia and Roy put the kitchen table over the main living room window. It'd be useless in keeping the beast out, but it made them feel better nonetheless. They left enough space for them to look outside. The creature had submerged, the *Europa* now reduced to floating wreckage. All their work, *everything*, was gone. Maybe some could be recovered with diving, but the computer notes, the hard drives, the paper documents, and specimens were gone.

Roy tapped his shoulder. "Let's just worry about survival."

Brett nodded. "You think that thing's gonna come up here?"

"Yes." There was no point in sugarcoating it. Roy knew it was just a matter of time. In fact, he was surprised the beast wasn't at the dock already. Perhaps it was searching the seafloor for any bodies that may have sunk.

"What about the Coast Guard?" Brett asked.

Roy took a moment to think about it. "Damn it. I don't know. I suspect the cutter is on its way back, but I never heard any confirmation. My only long-distance radio was on the boat."

"As was mine," Sicilia said. "I don't suppose anyone has a phone?"

"On the boat," Roy said.

"Mine too…" Brett muttered in defeat. He looked at Sicilia. "You don't have a radio in this house?"

"Needs to be replaced. Uncle Lucas never got around to it since nobody lived in this house for a few years."

"Is there a long-distance radio in his house?" Roy asked.

"Got damaged when the creature broke in," she replied.

"Fuck!" Brett kicked the door. "So, we can't call out for help. We have no boats, other than that skiff—like we'd get far in that. We can't run. There's nowhere else on this island to hide. To top it off, this beastie can pull apart this house like Legos."

"Relax, Brett. Don't lose your head," Sicilia said.

"She's right," Roy said. "We don't have a lot of options. Let's just fortify this place as best as we can, then come up with a few ideas. Keep in mind, the Commander was monitoring the traffic. He *has* to know something went wrong, especially now, considering that he's no longer getting traffic from his men. He's probably on his way back right now."

That helped. The thought of a Coast Guard cutter engaging that thing put Brett a little more at ease. "Hopefully, the crew will be on full alert."

"With the patrol unit radio silent, they have to assume the worst. We just need to wait out the next couple of hours." Roy leaned toward Brett. Though his assistant looked more relaxed, he still looked drastically uncomfortable. "You gonna be alright?"

"Yeah—I'll get to boarding up in just a sec. First, I gotta take care of something." He disappeared up the stairs and returned to the bathroom.

CHAPTER 21

Sicilia sipped on a glass of wine, which did little to calm her nerves. The wetsuit she wore felt tighter than ever. She pulled at the collar, which felt like it was trying to strangle her throat. She knew her senses were on overdrive right now. It was a natural characteristic when in danger.

Roy walked from window to window, peeping through the gaps of each one. So far, there was no sign of the beast. He returned to the living room to check the front window for what seemed like the hundredth time.

"Sit down, Roy," Sicilia said. "Have a drink. It'll help."

"I'm good," he said.

"I'm with her," Brett said. He had a whole bottle between his lips.

"One of us needs to stay on watch," Roy said. He checked his watch. Forty-five minutes had passed so far. He looked again, this time focused on the horizon. "Where the hell is that damn cutter?"

"They'll get here," Sicilia said. It was almost comical how the roles had reversed. Less than an hour ago, Roy was the one trying to calm *them* down. Now, though slowly, his nerves were getting the better of him.

Sicilia walked over to him, forced a wine glass into his hand, then filled it halfway. "Drink." Roy knew there was no point in arguing. He drank, reluctantly at first, then more enthusiastically…ultimately downing the whole serving. Sicilia smiled. "Wow, Doctor. If I didn't know any better, I'd say you were nervous for a date."

"If *I* didn't know any better, I'd say you were buttering me up," he retorted.

"If we get out of here—" she winked. The pleasurable thoughts worked wonders. Or maybe the wine was finally kicking in. She didn't care at this point. During the barricade, she explained what had happened with the Glasses and their nephew, Ricky. Though psychotic, those idiots were smart enough to use a more discreet boat to get their retribution. It was hard to admit that the monster had, in a way, saved her life. It was after telling that story when she realized she needed alcohol. She downed the rest of her own glass, then filled it back halfway.

"At this point, why don't you just drink from the bottle?" Brett said.

"Not a terrible idea, but no, I gotta keep some of my wits," Sicilia said. She sighed, then looked out the window at the dock. "Maybe it's injured. Those guys managed to hit it with that machine gun. Maybe it's dying from its wounds."

Roy nodded. "That would be a best-case scenario. I got a look at the bastard before I got off the boat. It was hurt. All the cutter needs to do is hit it with enough high-caliber rounds. They just need to concentrate a steady stream of bullets on its body. I saw its mantle. The flesh looks a little more rigid than its arms, but not impervious. It could be taken care of in a few seconds."

"IF they understood what they were up against," Sicilia said. "I don't know, though. That thing seemed to know exactly what it was doing. It knew how to prioritize its attacks, determine which vessel to strike first, and when to retreat."

"Cephalopods are intelligent creatures," Roy explained. "Modern day species have proven to have three times the neural wiring capacity than humans. And those species are *smaller* than humans. I can't imagine how intelligent this one is."

"We've outwitted it so far," Brett said.

"Even the smartest beings need experience to learn. My guess is that it only recently started hunting in shallower waters after being driven from its habitat by the toxic spill. It's not used to firearms and boats. I'll say this, the tricks we've used so far probably won't work again," Roy explained. "I'd say it's learned a lot from the recent attack. Probably why it's waiting. It's biding its time to make sure we don't have any tricks up our sleeves."

"So, you think it's prehistoric?" Sicilia asked.

Roy nodded. "That, or just an undiscovered subspecies. The ocean holds many mysteries. I'm starting to think some of them are best left undiscovered."

"Amen to that," Brett said. "Who knows. Maybe when it sees the cutter, it'll retreat. It wouldn't attack something *that* big. Would it?"

"I hope not." Roy didn't sound confident in his answer.

"You *hope*?" Sicilia stared him down for a more direct answer.

Roy wanted to keep it to himself to avoid further tension, but he was not a good liar. Not even by omission. "I'm afraid the opposite might happen. It might attack the cutter with increased ferocity. It knows how dangerous a forty-five-foot boat can be, and it knows it can take down a boat as large as the *Europa.* The cutter's not that much bigger."

"Still, it can't bite through the hull," Brett said. "I've seen the steel those ships are made of. Even something as strong as that octopus couldn't crush it."

"Maybe not, but it could drag it down into the water," Roy said.

Sicilia put her hand over her mouth. "You think it could pull that off? It's *that* strong?"

"If it's anything like its modern-day counterpart, then hell yeah it can. Some species are capable of lifting forty times their body weight. Assuming one that big has equal capabilities, then that cutter's in trouble."

Sicilia put the glass and bottle down. "If our only chance at rescue's not safe, then we need to do something ourselves."

Even for someone as knowledgeable as Roy Brinkman, it was hard to digest that fact. However, he couldn't deny the facts.

"That's our best bet. That said, I'm not exactly sure of what to do. It's not like we're armed to the teeth. All we have are a few knives, and no offense, but I'm not eager to go toe-to-toe with that thing."

"I don't think it has to go that far," she said. "We just need to figure out something else. You said yourself that it's smart but inexperienced. It might recognize a gunboat, but maybe not a land-based trap."

"What are you suggesting?" Roy asked. Sicilia led him to the back window and pointed to the propane tank on the northeast side of the property.

"If we can lure it close to the tank, we can rupture the gas, get a flame under it…I'm sure you can imagine the rest."

Roy felt his blood start to rush. "Risky, but it might work!"

"Uhh…" Brett stood up and pointed a finger, "I don't think so. We're lucky it hasn't already come after us. Maybe it's moved on."

"Fat chance," Roy said.

Brett threw his head back, frustrated. "You DO realize that to lure it, we'll need bait. *Live* bait. And in case you didn't notice, *we're* the only thing that qualifies."

"That's why I'm going," Roy said. That did little to make Brett feel better.

"Doc, you'll kill yourself. Let's just wait. Hiding has worked out well so far. We just need to get through the next hour or so. Someone will come.'

"And if that thing tears down our ride out of here?"

"Then someone ELSE will come. We'll just have to hide as best we can."

"Brett…" Roy walked over to his assistant. "You've studied the feeding habits of these things. What usually happens to prey that attempt to hide in a burrow when a cephalopod is after them?"

Brett thought for a moment. Just as he had done earlier for the doctor, Roy was using his knowledge of marine biology to snap him into reality.

"The cephalopod will continuously work on figuring out a way to drive the prey out."

"And…?"

"It almost always succeeds." Brett cleared his throat then wiped the sweat from his forehead. "Okay, I get the point. Let's blow the motherfucker up."

CHAPTER 22

They collected the dry logs from around the fireplace and grabbed a bottle of lighter fluid from the storage room. Sicilia tied sheets around the logs, which would soak better in the gas and hold a steadier flame.

Roy removed the barricades from the front door, then stepped outside. He noticed a few large ripples roughly a hundred feet offshore. Any lingering doubt about this course of action had now vanished. The beast absolutely was alive, and by the looks of it, it was on the verge of coming ashore.

"Sicilia, you have any tools?"

"In the shed," she replied. "Why?"

"I need to remove the intake valve, or else the flame will never touch the gas," he replied. "If I had a gun, I'd just shoot it." Sicilia looked at her revolver. Unfortunately, she spent all of her rounds during the escape, and the rest went down with the boat.

"Well, how are we gonna pull this off?" she asked. "It's not like you can open the tank and wait for the creature to approach. It could take several minutes. If too much propane escapes, then we won't get as big of a flame as we need."

"I know, I'm trying to think," he replied. She was right. On land, the monster may not be as fast. Yet, he couldn't stand next to the thing with a torch while he broke the seal. As much as he wanted to kill the beast, he wasn't keen on blowing himself up with it.

Time was running out. Brett pointed at the shoreline. The creature's mantle was briefly visible. It was moving in, though cautiously. Roy had been right about its wariness. It was deliberately drawing their attention to see if they'd try and fire any projectile weapons. Each time it showed itself, it was a little closer, though ready to flee. The octopus understood it was about to be in open terrain, fighting against land-based organisms. It would be without the cover of water.

"My God, that's fascinating," Roy said.

"Yes, it's great. We'll be on the front page of *National Geographic*. Now, can we figure out what to do?" Sicilia said.

Roy looked around. He envisioned throwing the hammer at the tank, but had the common sense to know that wouldn't do the trick. *God, why can't it be as easy as the movies make it look?*

"You sure you don't have any more bullets?"

Sicilia nodded. "The rest are in Uncle Lucas' house."

"Well fuck me! I'm gonna make a run for it, then!"

"No!"

"Si, we don't have a choice."

"I know. That's why *I'm* going," she said. "You don't know where he kept his belongings. I do, and we don't have time for me to explain it to you." A loud splash drew their attention to the shoreline. The creature had surfaced, its tentacles looking like the legs of a tarantula as it moved past the dock. It was officially making its attack. "Get the torches ready."

"Hurry up," Roy said. Sicilia never heard him, as she had already sprinted for the hill.

The marine biologist watched the creature haul its immense bulk to the shoreline. As he predicted, it moved rather slow on land, as it was unaccustomed to being out of the water. Despite this, it wasted little time advancing toward the hill. Already, it was clear that it would reach the house before Sicilia could. With no gunfire assaulting it, the beast grew increasingly confident.

"Shit!" Brett backed away from the door. "I knew this was a bad idea."

"Shut up, man. It was coming up regardless," Roy said.

"It'll be all over us by the time she gets back," Brett said.

"Let's light the torches, then," Roy said. "Get the matches." He soaked the ends of the torches with gas, then took the matches from Brett. He struck a flame and touched it to the wet fabric, which lit up into a dancing orange ball. He hurried to the door, saw the creature now halfway up the hill, then threw the torch like a tomahawk.

The burning end singed the soft fleshy webbing between the two front tentacles. The beast reared back, arms lashing at the strange hot object. It had never seen fire before, let alone felt the singe of its touch. The torch fell away and rolled down the hill, *under* its body. The octopus scurried to the side, then watched the bizarre glow of the torch.

As it faced the house again, another torch was thrown its way, striking it right below its left eye. Again, the beast flailed. It backed away, inadvertently crawling over the first torch.

Its tentacles lashed angrily at the ground, ripping up dirt and uprooting a couple of trees.

Brett swallowed. The decision to relieve himself earlier was a wise one, because he had no doubt he'd fail to hold it in now.

"I think you pissed it off."

As Sicilia descended the other side of the hill, she could hear the violent tearing of earth behind her. Now, more than ever, she was grateful for the slight buzz, otherwise she'd probably break down in a combination of guilt and terror.

Leaping over the glass fragments, she entered the house, then ascended the stairs. Uncle Lucas' gun cabinet was still open, the ammunition on the lower shelf. She grabbed a box, loaded six rounds into the cylinder, then ran back for the stairs.

She exited through the back door and sprinted for the hill. Suddenly, she was flung forward. She hit the ground hard, losing the boxes of ammo in the process. "Fuck!" She looked back, only to realize she had tripped over a cable that was linked to the house from the junction box in the island's center. Cursing repeatedly, she scampered around on her hands and knees and scooped up the ammo boxes, then sprinted up the hill.

When she reached the top, she saw the octopus ascending the hill. Roy was in the front yard, throwing another torch at it.

Its abhorrent smell filled the air, inducing a mild wave of nausea. The stomach-churning suctioning sound it made when out of the water didn't help matters. Sicilia sucked in a breath, then braved the rest of the journey.

"Hey!" she yelled to Roy. He saw her, then dove back into the house. The window nearest to the propane tank opened up, and the orange glow of a torch emerged.

"Lure it over!" he said. "When it's there, I'll toss the torch, then you shoot. Wait about five seconds so Brett and I can take cover on the other side of the house!"

The creature was at the top of the hill. Its mantle pulsated, dragging behind the web of tentacles like a potato sack. It closed in on the house, hardly taking any notice of Sicilia at all.

"Hey! HEY!!! Over here!" she shouted, waving her arms and jumping up and down to get its attention.

It didn't work. Tentacles lashed at the building, breaking glass, ripping out siding and insulation, and tossing the fragments into the yard. It tore at the ceiling, bringing huge slabs of wreckage over the front door and window.

Sicilia could hear the two men inside yelling and cursing. She waved her arms again to get the beast's attention, but it was too enthralled with the prey inside the house. Finally, she took aim and fired the gun, concentrating on the mantle.

The beast jerked backward, as a human would when stung by a bee. Sicilia fired another two rounds, pelting its face with lead. *Now* the cephalopod could see her. With slithery motions, it moved around the corner of the house. It moved faster than it did up the hill.

Sicilia backed away, making sure the propane tank was directly between it and her. The beast only had another twenty feet to go. She hoped Roy was ready at the side window, as she couldn't see from where she stood. The timing needed to be perfect. Now that the creature understood the burn of fire, they didn't want the torch thrown too early, which would likely result in the beast moving to the side or backing away entirely.

"Come on. Just a little further," she said. Its front tentacles slithered around the tank. Sicilia felt her heart race. The gun quivered in her hand. She could now see the smoke from Roy's torch coming through the window.

So could the creature.

It halted its advance, then with unexpected speed, it lunged at the house. Tentacles burst through the window, knocking the human behind it to the ground. The arm bent around the frame and pulled, effortlessly tearing a five-foot section of wall away. The other tentacles joined the fray, rapidly widening the gap.

Roy was on his back, having been struck by the appendage that penetrated the window. When he leaned up, he could see the creature's head and eyes. Suddenly, he was being pulled away from it. He looked over his shoulder at Brett, who dragged him by the back of his shirt.

"Get up, Doc!"

For the first time in his life, Roy hastily followed the instruction of his assistant. He stood up and ran, narrowly avoiding the reach of an outstretched tentacle.

They started to go around the back, only to see one of the tentacles right outside the door. With the front of the house caved in, there were no other avenues of escape.

"Upstairs," Brett said. It was a longshot, but he hoped they could find a window on the west side to jump from.

Within seconds, the whole side of the house was torn apart. The beast pressed its body into the gap, blindly reaching for the two humans who had retreated to the other side. It could sense vibrations of their footsteps, which echoed from the upper part of the house.

Like a spider, it pulled itself onto the roof. From there, it began peeling sections away.

Roy and Brett felt as though they were in the middle of a catastrophic earthquake. The house shook violently. The floor buckled and debris fell from the ceiling. All of a sudden, they saw sunlight streaming in where the roof had been.

Brett looked up and yelled. His decision to lead them upstairs was a bad one. The tentacle angled toward him, appearing for a moment as though it could 'see' him. Like a cobra, it sprang.

Roy grabbed his assistant by the arm while the tentacle looped around his body. A game of tug-of-war ensued for a brief moment. All it took was a heavy yank to heft its prey out of the house. Brett tried to scream, but the splintering bones slicing into his lungs prevented anything louder than a deathly gasp.

Sicilia fired the last three rounds at the creature. It seemed to take no notice of the lead that struck it beyond a brief jolt of pain. It didn't seem to consider her an actual threat at the moment. It simply played with its victim, waving him around in the air, before raising its body to stuff it in its mouth.

Even with all the destruction, the *crunch* was distinct, as was the blood that trickled from under the beast. Sicilia fell to her knees, defeated and horrified. The plan had failed miserably. Brett was now dead, with Roy soon to follow.

The octopus tore at the roof until nothing was left but a gaping hole. By now, there was hardly anything left to identify the building as a house. Her memories, her heritage, it was all ripped apart before her very eyes by this soulless demon of Earth's ancient past. All the money and recognition she had meant nothing now. She felt as poor as any of the homeless people she encountered in the inner cities. There was nobody left in her life. Her parents were dead, aunt, and uncle were all dead. She had no family, no real friends. She had nobody.

Except for Roy.

She heard him yell. The creature was reaching for him with its tentacles. She made a decision: she was *not* going to lose him too. There was only one other option, and that was to ignite the tank as planned. Considering the distance between it and the creature, it was unlikely the fire would spread far enough to kill it. However, it might be enough to drive it back into the water.

She saw smoke billowing from the wreckage that was once the east wall. Sicilia sprinted toward it, dug the torch out, along with some debris that had caught fire, then placed it by the propane tank. As she ran back, she ejected the empty cartridges from the revolver.

Roy made it down to the end of the hallway. Before he could take refuge in one of the bedrooms, he felt the end of a wet, slithery tentacle fold around his right ankle. It yanked back, literally pulling his feet out from under him, then dragged him across the floor before hoisting him into the air.

Swaying back and forth, he looked down at the beast. Those purple, bioluminescent eyes stared back with an expressionless gaze. It began to angle its body backward, lifting its mouth from the building. The beak extended, as did the horrific tongue.

Roy yelled in horror. In his many years of study, he had studied the feeding habits of cephalopods. During lessons in which he taught as an associate professor, he had joked about what a horrific death it would be. Never in a million years did he think he'd actually experience it.

Sicilia loaded fresh cartridges into the cylinder, and took aim. She tensed, prepping herself for the blast, then fired all six rounds into the propane tank. Lead punctured the metal shell, spewing propane gas into the fire. A fiery eruption followed. The huge tank spun like a top, whipping fire in all directions.

Tidal waves of flame swept over the house, singing the creature's rear tentacles. The sudden heat and pain caused it to drop its prey and scurry for safety.

Roy plummeted face-first into the house. Miraculously, he landed in Sicilia's bed. After seeing the fire consuming the wall behind him, he rolled to his feet and dashed into the hallway, ignoring the throbbing in his right ankle. He found the stairway and exited out the back door.

"Roy!" Sicilia cried out. He saw her backing away from the fire, which had engulfed the entire east side of the property, including part of the hillside. He ran to her side, then turned back.

They could barely see the monster through the wall of fire. But it was there, hurrying down the front yard. Part of its mantle and some tentacles were blackened, having been severely burned by the flames. The smell of smoldered flesh mixed with its natural stench.

It began moving to the left. After a few moments, Roy and Sicilia realized it was intently moving around the flame. Despite the heat and the pain it caused, the octopus was determined to get to them. Roy suspected it was acting out of vengeance at this point, as any other animal would have retreated into the water by now.

"It's one stubborn son of a bitch," he said. He clenched his fists, wishing that the creature would accidentally stumble into the flame. The sight of Brett being hauled to his death would forever haunt him. Any fascination he had for the creature was completely eradicated. He wanted it dead. Extinct. It was better that way. Next, he would see to it that the paper mill would suffer the penalties for drawing such a horrible lifeform from the depths.

First, they needed to survive this ordeal.

"Come on." He took Sicilia by the arm and guided her to the right. Predator and prey moved in a counterclockwise motion, the latter deliberately keeping the flame in-between them. By the time they reached the house, the creature was in the backyard. Realizing what they were doing, it quickened its pace.

As it did, a couple of its tentacles accidentally swept over a pool of fire on its left. The beast lurched in the opposite direction, coiling its arms back. It lashed about, as though trying to fight this bizarre enemy.

Roy and Sicilia seized the opportunity and sprinted for the hill. There was only one chance now: the skiff. Like marathon runners at the final stretch of the race, they reached the dock and hopped into the skiff.

The creature moved back along the peninsula hill, past the fire, and onto the slope of the front yard.

Roy started the motor and accelerated the boat southward. It moved excruciatingly slow. "Oh, for godsake!" he said. They were only three hundred feet out when the creature reached the shoreline. Like an arachnid with no exoskeleton, it crawled into the water, where it rapidly increased its pace.

He squeezed Sicilia's hand. She leaned against his shoulder. She was glad to get to know him in these last few moments. This last-ditch effort to escape was futile, but at least they were together.

"Weapons ready! Sixteen degrees port."

They turned toward the sound of the loudspeaker and spotted the USGSC *Horizon Flare* approaching at top speed. A gunman took manual control of the M242 Bushmaster autocannon at its bow.

Roy threw a fist in the air. "YES!" Capable of firing over a hundred .25mm rounds per minute, the autocannon would easily make minced meat of the octopus.

They could see Commander Rhea on deck with the megaphone in hand. They waved at him, and he back at them. "Turn to starboard and haul ass." He spoke in the same confident manner as before, as if battling kraken-sized sea monsters was an everyday occurrence.

"Don't have to tell me twice," Roy muttered.

CHAPTER 23

Commander Rhea watched the phenomenon through his binoculars. He couldn't believe it. That woman was telling the truth all along. He didn't blame himself: even the PhD didn't seem to believe it. Still, there was a reckoning to be had. This giant octopus had killed two of his men, and it would continue to kill unless it was put down.

He stood on the main deck, directing orders to the fourteen crewmen on his ship. Small arms were prepped, including two M60 machine guns which were set up on the port and starboard sides. The gun operator rotated the M242 Bushmaster to port, then centered the crosshairs at the target. There was disbelief in the young guardsman's eyes, and unlike Rhea, he couldn't hide it.

The beast was roughly twelve-hundred feet from the port bow, still in the shallow waters on the island's southern cove. However, what made Rhea nervous was how abruptly it had ceased its pursuit of the civilians. He wondered if the beast had sensed their presence. Unfortunately, in his twelve-years in the Coast Guard, he had never trained to deal with unidentified giant organisms. Nor did he have Dr. Brinkman on board to consult.

It wouldn't matter. That thing would be no match for the chain gun. That weapon was designed for penetrating the hulls of enemy ships and aircraft. No doubt it would make seafood out of this organism, even if it was enormous.

"Alright, gunner, let's get this over with." He got on his radio to communicate to the bridge. "Full stop."

The boatswain's call sounded off. The gunner turned the safety lever inward. He always thought if he would ever use the weapon outside of training, it would be against drug boats or pirates.

The com blasted across the deck. "Target moving to five-hundred yards."

"We're about to go live, Ensign," Rhea said.

"Aye-aye, sir."

The cephalopod was partially submerged, its eyes still above water, watching the new arrival. It had seen the large ship previously and had opted not to attack. Now, having gained experience in sinking these man-made crafts, it felt more confident in engaging this new foe. There was movement all along the top side, and it could see the pointed object at its front. It turned and pointed in its direction.

Memories flashed of similar pointed weapons used by the other vessel. It didn't understand the physics of them. All it knew was that they made a loud noise, and when they did so, it would feel the sting of some kind of projectile. During its combat today, it had learned that the larger weapons inflicted heavier damage. The little one held by the female barely penetrated its thick mantle, while the larger mounted ones inflicted more damage.

The weapon on the approaching ship was *much* larger. And it was pointed right at it.

The beast filled its mantle with seawater and jettisoned to deeper water. Right as it moved, the weapon unleashed its fury. Huge bullets struck its mantle, severing its siphon and shredding two of its tentacles. Its nervous system went on overdrive. The octopus squirted purple ink, which mixed with its trail of blood.

"It's on the go! Keep hitting it," Rhea ordered. The gunner rotated the weapon to port, firing off another dozen rounds into the target's trajectory.

"Target submerged. Visual lost," the spotter said.

"Give me a reading," Rhea said to the bridge.

The sonar operator's voice burst from the com. *"Sonar reading: biologic at one-three-five, portside. Steady on course. Range—nine-hundred yards."*

"Bring us around," Rhea ordered. The ship angled to port. Soon, the trail of ink and blood was dead ahead. The Commander crossed the deck as the ship turned, the starboard side now facing the area of conflict. He raised the glasses to check again on the civilians. They were keeping to the shallows, near the southwest bend of the island. It was obvious they were trying to keep close to shore; that way, if the creature double-backed, they could retreat on foot. It was fine with Rhea, as long as they remained out of the kill zone.

He looked to the south, seeing more ink and blook permeating the ocean. At first, it helped to track the thing's movements, but now the whole area was practically a giant black splotch. And it was getting darker. The once-clear water looked as black as his darkest nightmares.

"Give me an update. Is it still in the area?"

"That's affirmative, Commander."

He glanced about. He couldn't see an inch below the surface. The ocean may as well have been covered in some enormous black tarp. It would be impossible for the gunners to aim at the creature as long as it remained under the water.

"Smart bastard. Very smart indeed."

"It's circling about. Eight-hundred yards. Zero-four-five, portside."

Port?!

"Target moving northbound. Seven-hundred yards. Zero-nine-zero."

It was then that Commander Rhea fully understood that he wasn't dealing with a mindless animal. This was a creature capable of intelligent and strategic thought. It knew which sides were the front and back of the vessel, and which of those ends held the chain gun.

"Move the fifties to stern. If it attacks, it'll be from behind," he said. "Bridge, we have no visual. Water is too dark. We have to rely on that sonar. Increase speed to twenty-knots and bring us around again."

The vessel moved several hundred yards south, then proceeded to rotate in an attempt to put the chain gun in firing position. But the creature adjusted position, keeping either alongside or behind its opponent. As the ship initially circled around, the creature was briefly in firing range. The sonar operator announced its presence at forty-degrees port, still at seven hundred yards.

At Rhea's command, the gunman took his best shot, sending over a dozen yards into the target's approximate position. It was unclear whether they hit it or not, but the beast was alerted to the assault. It jetted, this time to starboard, quickly bringing itself alongside the *Horizon Flare.*

"Six-hundred yards, starboard. Five. It's closing in, Commander."

Rhea proceeded to the main deck. Both machine guns were now pointing off the portside.

"Four-hundred yards and closing. Speed increasing rapidly."

"If only we had explosives," Rhea muttered to himself. He watched the water, patiently waiting for the huge swells which would precede its arrival. A few seconds later, rolling waves materialized out of nowhere and struck the ship.

"Commence firing."

Both machine guns greeted the tentacles as they emerged from the surface. Fifty-caliber rounds shredded tissue, resulting in a hail of flesh and blood pelting the hull and deck.

The gunners whooped as they pressed the assault, one of them deliberately firing past the huge serpentine arms in hopes of hitting the head and mantle. As quickly as they arrived, the tentacles, now nothing more than minced, elongated pieces of meat, slipped under the water. They continued shooting for several seconds, until halted by their Commander.

"Visual lost," the spotter said.

"Position is One-eighty. Depth at one-hundred feet. It's coming up."

The creature arose behind an explosion of water. Two of its front tentacles were torn up, useless, attached to its body only by a few strands of flesh. One in the rear had been decimated by the Bushmaster. The other six, however, were still swift killing machines. They went right to work, lashing out onto the deck.

One snatched a guardsman by the torso and lifted him high into the air. The octopus was not interested in food at this point. This was about killing. It continued bending the arm around him, almost completely mummifying him. Then, with all its might, the creature squeezed. Bones turned to chips and organs imploded. Blood spilled from his body like cider from a crushed apple. The beast tossed the body into the water.

As this happened, another tentacle grabbed a guardsman, who was attempting to flee toward the structure. The tentacle snatched him by his left arm and yanked. With a *pop*, his arm detached from his shoulder, leaving an empty socket which sprayed blood on the deck.

The chaos created overwhelming confusion. The gunners rotated the Brownings to stern, though not in time to prevent the next action.

A tentacle stretched across the deck and snatched the nearest gunner by the waist. The guardsman screamed in agony as it waved him around like a kite. Suddenly, he was upside down, and returning to earth with the speed of a meteor. The tentacle slammed him to the deck, exploding his skull like a ripe melon. Brain and bone went in all directions like grenade shrapnel.

Rhea took control of the weapon and, along with the other gunner, opened fire on the creature. Tentacles coiled backward to protect its head, but not until several rounds found their way into the buccal mass. Other rounds tore into the tentacles and mantle for a brief moment before the beast fell back into the water. Blood, human and cephalopod, turned the deck bright red.

Before he could assess the situation, the water began to swirl. He heard a groaning of metal and felt the ship vibrate beneath his feet. He looked astern, watching the ocean seemingly moving to the left. The boat was rotating to starboard.

The rumbling intensified. The boat rocked slightly to port. An alarm sounded off. The rotation intensified. After a few moments, the stern was facing Diamond Green, then back out into the ocean. The creature literally had hold of the ship from underneath and was trying to pull it down. None of its arms were visible, meaning it was relying on its suction cups for grip.

"Break out small arms. Fire into the water. Use whatever we can to break its hold," he ordered the crew.

Guardsmen, armed with M16s, assembled on each side of the deck. Rifle shots filled the air, launching lead into the water in the vain hope of hitting the beast. Instead, all it seemed to accomplish was further its rage. The spinning of the ship intensified in speed. The bow started to dip and the ship leaned portside.

"Son of a bitch," Rhea muttered, barely keeping his voice down. Last thing the men needed to see was their Commander losing his cool. It took everything to keep that cool, however. The situation was going from bad to worse fast.

The Commander raced to the forward section. The riflemen on that side of the ship were still firing, but seemingly hitting nothing but ink-filled water. He opened his mouth to bark orders, only to stop at the sound of a splash.

A tentacle rose along the starboard side and slammed across the deck like a fist, pancaking a guardsman against the boat. Without hesitation, the tentacle slashed to the right, striking the Bushmaster and crushing its operator against the controls. It proceeded to wrap around the weapon, while another tentacle rose from the opposite side.

It lashed out like a whip, slashing a guardsman across the midsection. His body broke in two, both of which were flung across the air like golf balls, disappearing somewhere into the water.

The ship tilted. Rhea lost his balance and fell on his stomach. When he looked up, the Bushmaster broke from its platform and was raised high to the sky. He expected it to slip back into the water, but instead, it held position.

Then he realized the tentacle was bringing it down like a hammer—right on him. In his last moment of life, he finally lost his cool. His scream was as brief as the impact that crushed him.

The remaining tentacles finally emerged from the water and wrapped around the bow. With unmatched force, the beast pulled the vessel downward. Water rushed over the rail and across the deck.

More alarms blasted. The bridge crew announced for all hands to abandon ship. Not that they had any choice—they were ending up in the water voluntarily or not.

The ocean began flooding the lower decks, weighing the cutter down. With the ocean doing the rest of the work for it, the octopus stopped pulling in favor of climbing over the vessel.

One after another, it killed the remaining crew. Some were grabbed and squeezed. Others were battered against the ship like toys. One guardsman decided it would be best to end it quick by putting a pistol in his mouth and squeezing the trigger.

The octopus proceeded to attack the bridge, imploding it with a crushing squeeze, along with the crewmember who failed to evacuate. Meanwhile, the water spread across the lower decks. The *Horizon Flare*, still spiraling, quickly descended to its doom. Huge waves rolled in all directions as the vessel disappeared under a black ocean.

The octopus, injured but victorious, continued its assault until it was certain its enemy was neutralized. After several minutes, it backed away, exhausted and in pain.

It was feeling sluggish. The bullets had caused much internal damage. The big gun had hit its kidney and gonad, while the other, smaller-looking guns had severely injured its remaining tentacles and sinuses. The creature had no real concept of death beyond its instinct to eat and defeat enemies and predators. Though intelligent, it lacked the understanding that it could die of internal bleeding. It did understand, however, that humans were the ones that inflicted such harm. They destroyed its home, killed its food supply, and finally engaged it in direct combat. Now, only two remained.

The beast surfaced and saw the small boat on the shore. It was empty, its occupants having run inland once again.

It swam toward the island. The need to heal was secondary to its need to kill.

CHAPTER 24

Water splashed under their feet as the lovers leapt from the boat. With the cutter now gone, they knew remaining on the skiff was a death sentence, thus it was left lodged in the sand. They moved several meters up the beach before looking back at the frothing black water.

"My God," Roy said. The water was still swirling, as though a whirlpool was on the brink of formation. In the middle of it was the stern of the vessel. It twirled for another few moments before disappearing completely. After several more seconds, they heard it hit the seafloor.

"There," Sicilia said. She pointed a couple of hundred feet to the whirlpool. The octopus had surfaced and was staring right at them.

Roy closed his eyes and clenched both fists. "Can't we get one goddamn break?!"

"Come on," she said. "We gotta keep moving."

They started moving back to the island's interior, while keeping an eye on the monster's whereabouts. It was advancing to the shore, but rather slowly. It was undoubtedly injured by the Coast Guard's weaponry. Had they fired the Bushmaster a millisecond sooner, the thing would be a bloated corpse. But it had learned about its human opponents. It understood the threat of firearms. It also had come to learn about the threat of fire.

Roy looked to the big smoke cloud rising from Sicilia's property. "Let's go back. It won't come near the flames."

The trek was an annoying one, not because of the terrain, but the simple realization that they were literally going back and forth. Minutes ago, they were trying to *flee* the house, now they were actively going back. When they did arrive, the house was completely encased in flame. Soon, there would be nothing left. Maybe the smoke trail would alert help, but until then, they were on their own.

They got as close to the property as they could. The fire was blinding, the heat drawing sweat. They moved to the elevation between the property and Lucas', then looked back to the water. The beast was still out there. It was definitely watching them, but it was sluggish, and by the looks of it, reluctant to come up on land.

Sicilia looked at the burning house. "I'm gonna kill that bastard."

Roy looked at her. "Yeah? Got a bazooka you forgot to tell me about?" Not in the mood for humor, she didn't reply. Roy began to pace. She was right, as much as he hated to admit it. Escape was impossible. Boats that drew near were certainly doomed to the creature's wrath. It would take a helicopter to get them out of here.

Though it hesitated, neither of them doubted it would make landfall again.

"We need to set another trap," Sicilia said.

"With what?"

"Uncle Lucas has a propane tank behind his house. We could try the same strategy again," she said.

Roy shook his head. "It won't work. That thing will know what we're up to."

"You have a better idea?" she said.

He looked at the shed, which was barely out of the flame's reach. "Maybe." He ran over to it, pulled the doors open, and saw the gas grill in the back. Underneath it was a small propane tank. He disconnected it and checked the valve. Lucas had recently filled it.

He searched the shed for tools and a rag, which he found on an upper shelf, then stepped outside. He found a spot well beyond the reach of the flames, then knelt down.

"What are you trying to do?" Sicilia asked.

"I don't think it'll walk right toward the other tank, but we can toss this one at it like a Molotov cocktail. How good of a shot are you with that revolver?" he asked.

"I wouldn't call myself *Dirty Harry*."

"You think you could hit this tank? From maybe fifty feet out?"

Sicilia clenched her teeth and shook her head. "That's a tough shot for a novice like me. BUT...I might be able to pull it off."

They heard the splashing of water and saw the beast making its way ashore. It was slower, a few of its tentacles barely recognizable, and it was bleeding from its head and mantle. Despite this, it was still a vicious killing machine that could crush them in one coiling grip.

"I'm glad you're confident because we have no other option," he said. He dug through the tool bag and, to his relief, found a roll of electrical tape. He searched the ground for a piece of flaming debris that he could grab with his bare hands, then settled on a three-foot chunk of rafter which was only burning on one end. He strapped the clean end to the tank, then carried it to the top of the hill.

The creature crawled over the shoreline. It saw them standing just out of reach with the burning white tank in hand. That tank, while smaller, was similar to the last one that burst.

Roy swung the tank back and forth, garnering momentum for the big throw. Luckily, the hill would help gain distance. With the third motion, he tossed it with all its might, wincing as it hit the ground as he feared it would either burst on impact or that rolling down the hill would extinguish the flame. Luckily, neither happened. It rolled down the hill, settling a few feet ahead of the octopus' injured front tentacles.

Sicilia took a sniper position on her stomach. She extended the fully loaded revolver and cocked the hammer. With her elbows rested, she could more steadily center the tank in her iron sights. The beast remained still, aware of the small flame in front of it. She could only hope the fireball would be enough to finish it off.

She fired the first shot. Dirt kicked up to the left of the tank.

"Fuck!" She cocked the hammer and fired again. The dirt exploded a foot in front of the tank. A more seasoned marksman would've made the shot on the first try, but neither Sicilia or Roy had shot much in the last several years. If they understood anything beyond the basic mechanics, it was that it wasn't as easy as it looked in the movies.

"Steady. Relax…" Roy said. "You've almost got it." His calm demeanor broke as the creature began moving forward again. "Okay, make the fucking shot, would you?!"

Sicilia fired again. She heard a clang of metal. They both flinched, expecting the tank to erupt. Except it didn't. She had struck the handlebar near the valve. She was so close. However, she felt like she was getting the hang of it. She sucked in a breath, steadied her grip, and moved the iron sights ever-so-slightly to the left. This time, she *knew* she would hit the target.

She squeezed the trigger, expecting to see a big boom. Instead, she was lifted off the ground by Roy, who hastily pulled her away from the hill. Her bullet struck ground—the very ground the tank was lying on. The tank itself was launched into the air, having been swatted by one of the mighty tentacles. It struck the top of the hill with a crushing impact which fractured the tank, exposing the propane gas which ignited instantly upon touching the flame.

Sicilia's failure was their downfall. The creature understood what they were up to and not only foiled their plan, but used it *against* them.

Sicilia came to a halt when she heard Roy scream and fall to the ground. When she turned around, he was rolling about, his left leg completely covered in fire.

"Oh God! Roy!" she ran to his side and started batting the fire. Using the handle of her revolver, she raked up dirt and threw it over his leg. Roy scraped his leg against the ground. Gradually, they extinguished the flame, but not before it severely scorched the flesh on his calf and lower hamstring.

Sicilia saw the creature coming up the hill, moving around the newly created fire. She threw Roy's arm around her shoulder and lifted him to his feet. "Come on! We gotta go!"

Roy yelped with each step. His flesh rubbed against whatever was left of his pantleg and it was agonizing.

"Just go," he said.

"Shut up, damn you," she snapped. Out of desperation, she turned toward the creature and fired the last two rounds in her revolver. The creature jolted, then scurried backwards, tentacles lashing about. For once, they actually did have a stroke of luck; one of her bullets struck the tattered flesh which protected its buccal mass. Nerves lit up like lightning bolts, buying them a few extra seconds to get ahead.

Sicilia led Roy to Lucas' property. He was shaking his head in defeat.

"Si, just let it take me. I'll use myself as bait, while you get away. Use the skiff! It's a long shot, but you might be able to make enough distance while it tries to get at me."

"No. You're all I have left," she said.

He made a pained laugh. "Girl, we've only known each other for twenty-four hours. You talk like we're destined to be married after this."

"I can think of worse outcomes," Sicilia replied. She shrugged. "Uncle Lucas and Aunt Mary were love at first sight. I suppose such a thing is possible. Then again, maybe it's just a survivor's instinct: focus on the good and use it as fuel to escape the predicament you're in. Then again, I suppose you don't feel the same way…"

He turned and pressed his lips to hers. The kiss lasted several moments, after which he leaned his forehead against hers. "Let's make sure there's a few dinner dates before we jump right into the marriage part."

She smiled. "Deal."

They could hear the beast moving on the other side of the peninsula again. They couldn't see it, but there was no doubt it would be at the top of the hill within a few moments.

"I don't suppose you have any ideas?" she said.

"All I can think of is the propane tank, and that's doomed to fail," Roy said. "The thing is wise to our plan. The only thing we can trap it with is something it's unfamiliar with."

"Something it's unfamiliar with…" Sicilia was thinking out loud. Her eyes went to the junction box northwest of the property. "What about electricity?"

Roy looked over at it, then shook his head. "In theory, yes, that would kill it. But you'll never get the bastard close enough without frying yourself along with it. You need bait." He held his arm out. "Don't know about you, but I don't see anything we can bait the trap with."

Sicilia's eyes widened. "Yes there is."

"What?" Roy asked.

"If I told you, you'd try and talk me out of doing it…and we don't have that kind of time. Come on!"

She led him to the shed, where she dug out some of Uncle Lucas' diving supplies. He had a fresh scuba tank, rebreather, and goggles. In addition, there were a couple of spearguns on the side. Spearfishing was a joy that ran in the family. She grabbed both and loaded a spear into each of them, then pulled some rope from the top shelf. She examined the inch-thick line, and tested it with a few sharp tugs. "This'll do."

"Do for what?!" Roy asked, alarmed.

"No time to explain. Hide in here and don't make a single sound."

"Si, whatever you're planning to do, think about it twice, and then DON'T DO IT!"

She pulled him in for a kiss, shutting him up, then forced him back into the shed. With his injured leg, he offered little resistance. The door slammed shut, and he heard her take off running.

"Women," he muttered.

Sicilia dashed up the hill, then spotted the creature. She threw her hands about and shouted. "Hey! Over here, you Japanese cuisine!" The beast turned its attention from Lucas' property over to her. Tentacles flailed about, eager to grab ahold of her and crush her until she was as limp as a wet rag.

She backed away, making sure its attention was fixed on her. It proceeded to follow. Its injuries provided an advantage she desperately needed. It was slower, granting her the ability to keep it at a distance. And its bloodlust prevented it from ravaging her uncle's property in search of Roy. It would search for him later. For now, it wanted to kill this human who flaunted a projectile weapon.

"Yeah, come on. You think you're the only fat bastard who thought they had the best of me? You should see my ex-husband. Even uglier than you, that fucker is." She increased her pace. "I escaped his clutches. I'll escape *yours*."

She whipped around and ran as hard as she could for the northwest beach. She could hear the crushing of vegetation and hard ground as the beast quickened its pace. Still, its injuries kept it at sluggish pace, giving its prey the advantage of escape.

But it wasn't escape Sicilia sought. As she neared the beach, she looked for the black cable.

There!

She followed it to the shoreline, then quickly threw on her diving gear. She did a brief test with her rebreather, then raced into the water, with the rope slung over her shoulder. She would have to act fast. The monster would be much faster underwater than on land.

CHAPTER 25

With one speargun slung over her shoulder and the other pointed forward, Sicilia followed the cable to the depths. She watched the world in front of her, watching for any moving shapes. At the same time, she waited for any strong vibrations behind her. The beast had not entered the water yet. It was probably unaccustomed to humans swimming deep. It was possible it was confused and waiting for her to surface.

Good. Buys me another couple of minutes.

After another hundred feet, she found the ledge where she encountered the shark. Right at her feet was the patch of weeds where she snagged her feet on the wire.

Where are you?

She gently lowered herself off the ledge and followed the forty-five degree angle slope of line, careful not to get too close to any coral. Something moved in the distance, but she quickly lost sight of it. She made a few frantic motions, mimicking wounded prey. She rolled around, thrusting her arms, while being careful to not lose her spearguns or rope.

Finally, the shark came into view. It moved gracefully towards her. At a hundred feet, it turned away and started gliding to the north. Sicilia thrashed about more, but the fish didn't seem to care. Perhaps the shark, despite being hungry and desperate, learned to avoid humans after their last encounter.

Shit!

Anxiety struck Sicilia's nerves like a hurricane. For her special plan to work, she needed bait suitable for the octopus to grab with a tentacle. And there it was, the perfect bait, but it was out of reach.

There was a rush of water coming from behind her. She turned around, seeing some of the bleached coral waving to the west. The thing had finally entered the water.

Sicilia closed her eyes and inhaled deeply. In that moment, she allowed herself to be in a meditative trance.

Her mind focused on good memories. She was on the kitchen couch, holding a glass of wine, in complete bliss as she listened to the new man in her life tell his stories of working in the ocean.

"I decided to take my diving knife and to draw a little blood to direct one of the bad boys closer to me. Let's just say, it worked, but almost too well. Had to let go of the tuna before it even got near because, had I held on any longer, I would've lost my hand along with the fish. The shark came so hard, it knocked us both to the other side of the cage."

Sicilia opened her eyes. The shark was still in the distance, swimming slowly, uninterested in her. She drew her diving knife and extended her left arm. Slowly, she made an incision along her forearm. Surprisingly, she didn't feel much pain from it, probably thanks to the adrenaline. The sight of her own blood clouding in the water was unsettling. But it worked.

The starving shark immediately detected the scent. Its speed doubled, its snout now pointed toward her. Any reservation it had about attacking the human was gone. The smell of blood in the water was too enticing, especially for a creature that had gone without a meal as long as it had.

Sicilia took aim with the speargun and awaited its approach. *I'm sorry.* Even now, after all the pain and terror, even after the shark's previous attack, she took no joy in what she was about to do. It needed to be done, though.

The shark came within thirty feet, doubling its speed once more. Sicilia squeezed the trigger. The spear zipped from the weapon, punching through the shark's snout, right above the upper jaw. The shark spiraled like a jet fighter, blood spurting from its head. Yet, it kept coming.

Sicilia thrust the speargun out, holding it horizontally to block the jaws. The shark plowed into her, driving her backward against the rock wall. It bit down on the speargun and yanked it from her hands.

It turned away, spitting out the inedible object, then circled back around for another bite. Sicilia drew her knife, then pushed her feet against the rock wall, launching her up at a forty-five degree angle. The shark passed under her, clumsily striking the rock, stunning itself. Sicilia turned around to face it.

As she did, she noticed movement a little to the south. It was like watching a moving mountain under the water. The beast was out there, searching for her. She watched it turn, spurred by the scent of blood and vibration caused by the struggle.

She had a minute at best to set the trap. She drew her knife again and closed in on the shark. It angled its jaws toward her, ready to rip a chunk out of her midsection. But the injury to its head compromised its depth proception, as well as make it increasingly sluggish. Sicilia was able to keep out of reach by pressing her palms against its snout.

She raised the knife high and brought it down on its head. She pushed it down as hard as she could, like driving a nail through a board. The blade sank into the shark's brain. It spasmed as the life drained from it, then proceeded to twitch.

Even now, Sicilia felt no joy or even relief from the victory. She lassoed the rope around its pectoral fins and dragged it toward the cable, watching the octopus advance from a few hundred feet beyond.

She pulled down on the cable, then looped the rope between it and the shark's body. It was still twitching, the last electrical impulses of life still surging from its brain.

You're saving the reef, she wanted to tell it. *This beast that carried man's pollution to our home, you are the one who'll bring an end to it.* Maybe that was God's plan. Maybe the attack yesterday was something she was *meant* to experience. Maybe that inner drive to come home was a message in her heart. Maybe, she wasn't meant to reunite with her uncle. Maybe she was meant to save Diamond Green.

She looped the rope repeatedly, then tightened it into a noose, squeezing the shark and the cable together.

By the time she finished, the beast had closed to eighty feet of distance. Its tentacles were almost within reach. Its mantle rose high, the functional arms coiling outward, taking the pose of some horrifying arachnid. Purple eyes gazed down at the human, one final glance before it would have the satisfaction of killing her.

Sicilia unslung the second speargun and pointed it at the beast.

For Uncle Lucas...for Diamond Green.

She launched the spear, which struck the creature in the corner of its right eye. Tentacles slashed the water as the beast writhed in fury.

It took everything for Sicilia to focus. She wanted to run, but knew she needed to stay, or else it would proceed to chase her. She pressed herself to the bait, keeping the creature's attention on her. She removed her scuba tank, then flipped it upside down. She slipped her arms back into the harness, putting it on backwards, putting the tank in front of her. She wrapped one arm around it, while holding the handle of her knife out like a hammer.

For the next few moments, she waited. The creature advanced with a fury. Its tentacles coiled back like cobras, ready to strike.

Sicilia struck the valve. The end of the tank burst, rocketing her to the surface right as the arms lunged. The beast found flesh, but it wasn't human flesh. The creature its tentacle grabbed was nearly dead, and was leaking blood from its head and gills.

Food was food.

Sicilia broke the surface. Immediately, she felt the squeezing headache from improper recompression. She ignored the pain and redirected the rocketing scuba tank toward shore, as she didn't want to be in the water during an electric surge. The stretch of blue between her and the white-tan sand disappeared in the blink of an eye.

She hit the shallows and was flung forward. She bounced head-over-heels before ultimately settling in three feet of water. She felt the sting of saltwater in her eyes, then realized the mask had slipped off. She tried to stand up, but her body worked against her. It felt like her skull wanted to split open. Her body was like a wet noodle. She was so close to shore, yet so far.

A shout of pain filled her ears, followed by the sound of splashing. A pair of arms picked her up by the shoulders and dragged her to shore.

Next thing Sicilia knew, she was lying on the sand, gazing up at Roy Brinkman.

The beast lifted the shark to its mouth. There was slight pullback. The food seemed to be attached to something. No matter. The beak would easily slice through the object…

The beast chomped.

It saw a flash of white, and suddenly, the creature convulsed. Ten-thousand volts of electricity surged through its body, frying its tongue and beak, and stopping all three of its hearts. Tentacles froze in rigid formations, while the mantle shook furiously. Finally, the hearts burst. Only death and gravity separated the octopus from the wire.

Roy and Sicilia watched the white flashes, which resembled underwater lightning in the distance. After several tense seconds, it all came to an abrupt stop.

Sicilia leaned her head against Roy's shoulder. He wrapped his arms around her and held her close. The warmth he felt overcame the pain in his leg.

"You're one crazy woman," he said.

She rubbed her hand against his. "Runs in the family."

"Well, I guess it's a good thing I like crazy," he replied. She smiled. Over the next several minutes, they remained on the beach together. Finally, something emerged in the distance. The charred, bloated body of the cephalopod rolled with the waves, the tentacles making squiggly lines as the waves lapped against them. The mantle looked like a deflated balloon lined with spikes, and full of fleshy tears. The purple eyes were now black.

The Monster from the Abyss was dead.

CHAPTER 26

ONE YEAR LATER

Sicilia Brinkman smiled, watching the abundance of life flourish all around her. Fish of all different species swam about. Some fed off the coral, while others made shelter. The pasty white dead coral had withered away, making way for new, healthy coral. Looking around her, she didn't see a single patch of white, except for the underbellies of some fish. Further to the west, mako sharks, hammerheads, and reef sharks glided amongst the crowd. Not one of them looked malnourished or sickly.

There was no speargun in her hand. She didn't need one.

The water was crystal clear, allowing her eyes to feast on the vibrant colors the reef had to offer. It was just like she remembered from her childhood. Better even. It was healthy, flourishing, untouched. And untouched it would remain. That was the rule of the Lucas Instone Sanctuary.

A hand tapped on her shoulder. She turned around and saw her newlywed husband. He had six vials of water taken from various spots on the seafloor. She held up the samples she had taken from around the North Peak.

Yes, hon. I'm a good assistant.

She could see him smiling under that mask. It would be the last test before confirming the dioxin levels around Diamond Green had dissipated.

Together, they surfaced, then boarded their vessel, the *Brett Rollins.* After placing the samples into the lab, they gazed at the island together. Diamond Green, now known as the *Lucas Instone Sanctuary for Sea life*, would live on to be more beautiful than ever before. Fishing was prohibited for a mile on each side, with special buoys marking the perimeters.

"Never thought I'd spend my honeymoon working," Roy joked.

"Work isn't work when you're in paradise," Sicilia said.

Roy smiled. "No, I suppose it's not."

They embraced each other. The only thing they found more beautiful than a clean ocean was each other.

Check out other great

Sea Monster Novels!

Michael Cole

CREATURE OF LAKE SHADOW

It was supposed to be a simple bank robbery. Quick. Clean. Efficient. It was none of those. With police searching for them across the state, a band of criminals hide out in a desolate cabin on the frozen shore of Lake Shadow. Isolated, shrouded in thick forest, and haunted by a mysterious history, they thought it was the perfect place to hide. Tensions mount as they hear strange noises outside. Slain animals are found in the snow. Before long, they realize something is watching them. Something hungry, violent, and not of this world. In their attempt to escape, they found the Creature of Lake Shadow.

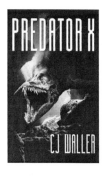

C.J. Waller

PREDATOR X

When deep level oil fracking uncovers a vast subterranean sea, a crack team of cavers and scientists are sent down to investigate. Upon their arrival, they disappear without a trace. A second team, including sedimentologist Dr Megan Stoker, are ordered to seek out Alpha Team and report back their findings. But Alpha team are nowhere to be found – instead, they are faced with something unexpected in the depths. Something ancient. Something huge. Something dangerous. Predator X

SEVERED**PRESS**

@severedpress
/severedpress

Check out other great

Sea Monster Novels!

Matt James

SUB-ZERO

The only thing colder than the Antarctic air is the icy chill of death... Off the coast of McMurdo Station, in the frigid waters of the Southern Ocean, a new species of Antarctic octopus is unintentionally discovered. Specialists aboard a state-of-the-art DARPA research vessel aim to apply the animal's "sub-zero venom" to one of their projects: An experimental painkiller designed for soldiers on the front lines. All is going according to plan until the ship is caught in an intense storm. The retrofitted tanker is rocked, and the onboard laboratory is destroyed. Amid the chaos, the lead scientist is infected by a strange virus while conducting the specimen's dissection. The scientist didn't die in the accident. He changed.

Alister Hodge

THE CAVERN

When a sink hole opens up near the Australian outback town of Pintalba, it uncovers a pristine cave system. Sam joins an expedition to explore the subterranean passages as paramedic support, hoping to remain unneeded at base camp. But, when one of the cavers is injured, he must overcome paralysing claustrophobia to dive pitch-black waters and squeeze through the bowels of the earth. Soon he will find there are fates worse than being buried alive, for in the abandoned mines and caves beneath Pintalba, there are ravenous teeth in the dark. As a savage predator targets the group with hideous ferocity, Sam and his friends must fight for their lives if they are ever to see the sun again.